The Storyteller of Cottage H

The Storyteller of Cottage H

E. E. "Doc" Murdock

H.O.T. Press
Publishing fine books since 1983

H.O.T. Press
Los Angeles, California
www.hotpresspublishing.com

ISBN: 0-923178-37-6
ISBN-13: 978-0-923178-37-6

Books by E.E. "Doc" Murdock

Novels

- **The Robots of Cottage H**
- **God's Messenger – God's Victim**: A *Bildungsroman* Stockholm Syndrome Novel
- **The Pain Artist:** An American Hikikomori
- **My Vietnam War**
- **A Psalm for Cock Robin**: A Harp and His (Dead) Mother Mystery
- **Crueltown**: A Drew Steele Los Angeles-Las Vegas Mystery
- **The End of the Civil War**: A Drew Steele Civil War Mystery
- **Who Owns Arizona**: A Drew Steele Civil War Mystery

Textbooks/How-To Books

- **How to Write Fiction: Tools and Techniques**
- **Self Management: A Guide to More Effective Study**
- **Computers Today**
- **Computers the Easy Way**
- **Windows the Easy Way**
- **DOS the Easy Way**
- **HyperCard the Easy Way**
- **dBASE the Easy Way**

History/Political Books

- **From Washington and Adams to Hillary and Trump:** The Stories behind the Story of Every Presidential Election, With Special Focus on the *Volatile* Presidential Election of 2016

- **Obama Won, but Romney Almost Was President:** How the Democrats Targeted Electoral College Votes to Win the 2012 Presidential Election

Acknowledgments

I am indebted to the members of the Ojai Writing Workshop who provided valuable feedback as I worked through the many drafts of this book. I would also like to acknowledge the help of all my students at California State University, Long Beach who taught me so much. And of course, in the end, it was Zoe that made this book happen.

For Zoe,
without whom this book would not exist,
and without whom I would not exist.

One

Waiting for the results of the draft lottery drawing, I didn't do much all summer except read bad novels and watch worthless TV nonsense. It felt like I was waiting for a jury to come back with my death sentence, which in this case, would have been a registered letter from the U.S. government saying, in more or less official-sounding language, "You are sentenced to be drafted and sent to Vietnam to probably get yourself killed." But my birth date was not one of the ones drawn, so I guess I might as well go ahead and get registered for another semester at the university.

I drive to the U and head for the gymnasium to start the arduous registration process. I pick up a registration form and get in the long line. After waiting for about forever in the stupid long line they make you wait in just to start the process, I finally make it to the sign-in desk. I hand the woman behind the desk my registration form.

She glances at it and points to where I'd listed my major as "undeclared. "You can't be undeclared," she says. "This is your third year."

"Third year? Why does that matter?"

"Third year, third year," she says even more impatiently. "You have to declare a major."

Starting my third year means I have to declare a major? Why didn't anybody tell me that? "Uh," I say, "I need to think about it."

"Then get out of line," she says and tries to look past me.

No way I'm going to wait in that ridiculously long line again, so I say, "Okay, make it . . . uh, psychology."

She crosses out "Undeclared" and writes in "Psychology." She hands me back my form, looks past me, and says, "Next."

I head for the next set of long lines at the course registration tables. What did I just do? Psychology? I've only taken one entry-level psychology class. It was interesting, but nothing that would make me want to become a psychologist. If I end up with a degree in psychology—assuming I don't get drafted first—will it in any way prepare me for what I want to do in life?

Ah, but that's the real question, isn't it? What do I want to do in life? I have no idea. I've just been *being* a college student. And before that I was just *being* a high school student. No plan, no real hopes for the future, just *doing it*.

But I do have to admit I'm lucky to still be able to be a college student. My father's death settlement from the asbestos class action lawsuit not only left my mother enough money to send me to college, she also pays for a small apartment near the university. Actually, it's what they call a "studio" apartment—one room with a small fridge, a counter-top stove, a couch/bed that's pushed up against the wall next to the tiny bathroom. My mother agreed to keep paying the rent, *as long as I stay in college.*

Anyhow, I guess being required to declare a major might be a good thing. Maybe more focus is just what I need. My father took a long time to die, and I felt like I shouldn't be doing selfish stuff like going out with *my* friends, when *he* was the one who needed a friend. We did everything together. His big thing was hunting and fishing, so that became my big thing too. Just the two of us, always out in nature, fishing and hunting. In time, he became my only friend.

But since he died, I haven't touched a fishing rod, and the idea of shooting something to make it dead, completely sickens me.

My father's death pushed me down into such a sad place, I don't really like to talk to anybody. I've been pretty much just staying by myself, trying to get over losing him. I've just been taking random college classes, going through the motions of being a student.

So maybe I really did need to decide on some kind of new direction in my life. Maybe by taking some psychology courses and learning about mental processes, I'll learn more about my own mental processes. Maybe it will help me get over my father's death and move on with my own life.

I finally get through the rest of the registration process, signing up for just a few psychology courses. I leave the building, but halfway to my car, I stop. I can't quite face going back to my apartment. What would I do there? Eat crappy food and watch pointless TV? No, what I should do is go to the psychology building. Maybe there I can get a feel for what it will like to be a psychology major.

After walking the halls of the psychology building for a while, I'm still not really getting any idea of what it will be like to be an actual psych major.

Walking past the psychology department office, I stop to look at a glass case with notes and bulletins related to psychology department stuff. One of the notices says upper-division psychology majors can get three credit hours of independent study by signing up for an on-site "experience." That sounds good to me. Three upper-division credit hours for doing something psychology related. Might as well jump right in and get used to being a real live psych major.

I go into the office and the lady there signs me up for it. She tells me to just show up at the local mental hospital next Monday morning. She gives me the address of the hospital and says they'll tell me what my assignment there will be. "Uh," I say, "what are the requirements? Will I have to write a report or . . . something?"

She says, "Probably. We're still working that out."

I walk out of the office wondering what she meant by "still working that out." It must be some kind of brand new program. Am I the first one to sign up for it?

As I walk, I stare at the address she wrote on the paper. Nothing on the paper but the handwritten address of the mental hospital where I'm supposed to go Monday morning. But what am I going to be doing there?

Oh well, I guess I'll find that out when I get there.

The fact that I know absolutely nothing about mental health treatment should make me really nervous about visiting an actual mental hospital.

But maybe I'll just be some kind of remote observer.

But what if they give me some kind of job? When I

signed up for this independent study "experience," I was only thinking it would be an easy way to get three hours of upper-division credit, but now that I'm thinking through it, I'm wondering if it might not turn out to be more complicated. Aren't mental patients dangerous? What if I get locked inside a ward with a bunch of dangerous mental patients? What have I got myself into?

Two

My first class at the university isn't until tomorrow, so my first experience as a psych major will be today at the mental hospital. Driving up the narrow curving driveway that leads up to the hilltop mental hospital, I see that the facility seems to be made up of several red-brick buildings. I wonder if those buildings are the individual wards.

A sign says there's a staff parking area and a visitor parking area. I hesitate. I decide to park my old car in the visitor's lot. It's the only car in the lot. Don't the patients at this place get any visitors?

There's a large brick building close to the parking lot. That must be the administration building. It looks real old, with some kind of fancy stone cornice all along the front edge of the roof. It sort of looks like a castle—if they would have made castles out of brick—and it has what looks like a bell tower up on top. No bell inside though. Maybe, at one time, the old building used to be a church.

The sun is barely above the eastern horizon, and I don't quite feel like going in just yet, so I stay in my car. In fact, I'm wondering if I really want to do this. The old brick building seems kind of somber and foreboding, sort of like that terrible place they put my father in for his last six months. Maybe signing up for this "experience" wasn't such a good idea. What if the patients are violent? And how will they know I'm just a student visitor and not a new patient? Could a person accidentally get locked up in a place like this and never be heard from again?

But why am I getting so nervous? Surely they'll give me some kind of uniform to let everybody know I'm not a patient. I've got to stop letting those kinds of negative thoughts deter me. All I have to do is keep my head down, do whatever it is I'm supposed to do, and the semester will be over before I know it. I'll just walk right in there, tell them I'm the university student, and ask what I'm supposed to do. Nothing to be nervous about.

I get out of my car and go into the building like I know exactly what I'm doing. Just inside the door, an older woman, wearing a guard-type uniform, is sitting behind a desk. She listens to my explanation of why I'm there and tells me to wait. She makes a brief phone call.

As I wait, she stares at me. She's got to be sixty, at least, with scraggly gray hair and what looks to be a permanent frown.

Why is she staring? Is she suspicious of me?

I need to stop thinking like that. She's probably only staring at me because she doesn't have anything else to look at.

I ignore her and look around. Nothing on the walls. No pictures of anything. But up high on the far wall is what seems to be a stained-glass window. Too dirty to see what it might depict though. It again makes me wonder if this building used to be some kind of church.

Finally, a middle-aged woman in a white nurse's uniform comes down the hallway toward me.

I tell myself all I have to do is act like a normal student. And be cheerful.

I stick out my hand and cheerfully say, "Hello. I'm the psychology student from the university."

She doesn't smile as she says, "I know who you are." She hands me a badge that has the words "STUDENT-VISITOR" printed on it. Under that is my name, handwritten. She says, "You must wear that badge at all times."

Thank goodness. A badge. Now there'll be no mistaking me for a patient.

The nurse-type person doesn't say another word. She just looks me over.

She also doesn't seem very friendly. Maybe they don't like outsiders here.

But I can't let those kinds of thoughts deter me. I should just go with the flow. That's what my father used to tell me. It doesn't matter if this nurse-type person is friendly or not. I'm here, and I'm going to be here for the whole semester. I'll just focus on the three credit hours of independent study credit I'm getting and try to learn something about the psychology of mental patients.

As I'm pinning the badge onto the lapel of my tweed jacket with the cool leather patches on the elbows, she says, "Nice jacket."

Was that a hint of sarcasm in her voice? What's wrong with my jacket? She can't know that I just bought it for five bucks at the local thrift store on Saturday, can she?

Maybe she really does think it's a nice jacket. I bought it special for today so I could look at least a little bit "professional" for this student "experience."

And who cares what she thinks anyhow? I have a perfect right to be here, and as a student, I can dress any way I want to.

She says she'll give me a "walk-through" that will introduce me to the facility. Then, she turns on her heel and starts walking away from me. She doesn't say "Let's go," or anything. She seems impatient, and she hasn't even introduced herself. Is this the way it's going to be here? Unfriendly and impolite? Maybe I should just go back to the university and tell them I changed my mind.

No, damn it, I've got to stop thinking like that. I'm not going to turn tail and run. This is supposed to be a useful experience for psych majors. I should just take advantage of it and not let it bother me if the people here are unfriendly to students.

I hurry to keep up with her as she leads me out of the administration building onto a wide sidewalk. Some weeds are growing in the sidewalk cracks. That seems odd. Don't they have anybody to take better care of this place?

I should probably stop analyzing everything. Better to just go along to get along; that's what my father would have told me to do.

My nurse-guide is leading me on, not saying a word.

Maybe I should be asking questions, or saying something friendly, no matter how impolite she is.

But I can't think of anything to say, and hopefully this will be the only time I'll ever have to deal with her. I'll just follow along and keep my mouth shut. Before he died, one of the last pieces of advice my father gave me was, "Keep your eyes open and your mouth shut, and you'll do fine." Lying there in that narrow bed at the so-called *care* facility, he was almost too weak to get the words out, but I could tell he wanted to tell me a few things like that before it was too late. After that session of advice-giving, he didn't talk much anymore; I could tell he was ready to get the dying part over and done with.

Not surprising that this old mental hospital reminds me of that place; it's just about as old and worn out. In the six months it took him to die in that place, I came to hate it. Long-term *care* facility my ass. There was no care going on there. Warehouse for the dying was more like it, with staff that was just as impatient as this nurse that's guiding me here. Maybe this place is like that place, a warehouse for mentally ill people. But they must get some kind of treatment here, don't they?

My guide stops in front of the first brick building we come to. She takes out a ring of keys and says, "We'll start with the men's intake building." She unlocks the door and leads me down a hallway that was painted gray a long time ago. It leads to a large room where a few men are sitting in large gray fake-leather chairs with chrome armrests. She says, "These men are waiting to be evaluated. Then, they'll be assigned to a ward."

The men don't look very happy. I decide not to look at them too closely. They might not like it, and they might be dangerous. But then, none of the men are restrained in any way, and only a few of them even bother to look up at us as we pass through, so maybe I'm getting all worried needlessly.

I wonder why these men ended up in a place like this. They all look pretty normal to me. None of them are acting. . . well, crazy. But then, what did I expect, that they would be running around screaming or something?

We leave the building by the same front door, and she takes me to yet another brick building. Inside, I see that it's a gymnasium with a worn hardwood floor that has faded lines that show it might have once been used as a basketball court. No basketball hoops though.

"For recreation therapy" is all she says.

I wonder why there are no patients in the building. In fact, it looks like the place hasn't been used for a long time. Don't they do recreation therapy anymore? And we still haven't seen any patients walking around. Maybe, in this kind of institution, the patients are always kept locked up. Obviously, I don't know anything about mental health treatment, but just keeping them locked up doesn't seem like a very good idea.

The next brick building we come to is much smaller. Inside, a hugely overweight teacher is teaching a small group of teenagers basic math by writing simple addition and subtraction formulas on a blackboard. Finally, some actual patients, and somebody trying to help them.

The huge man that's doing the teaching makes eye contact with me, smiles, and nods.

I don't know how I'm supposed to respond, so I just nod back.

He goes back to teaching.

Why would they have young people in a place like this, especially such normal-looking kids? Seeing kids here doesn't seem quite right, given how old and worn out the whole hospital looks.

After we're back outside, I ask my guide, "What ages are in residence in this institution?"

She simply says, "Teen to whatever."

Okay, at least there are no young children here. I'm not sure how I would deal with that.

She hurries me along to what she says is a "treatment building."

In the first room, there are several large, old-looking, bath-tubs with canvas covers. She says the tubs are used for "hydrotherapy."

I wonder if the patients are put into water and kept in the

darkness under those thick canvas coverings. A scary thought.

My guide hurries me out of that room, so I decide against asking her about that.

Still no patients around. If this is the "treatment" facility, where are the patients? So far, I haven't seen one bit of actual treatment going on.

Next, she takes me into what she says is the "electroconvulsive therapy room."

It's a small room with a narrow hospital bed in the center. Next to the bed is some kind of electronic device on a wheeled cart. That must be the device that delivers the electroconvulsive therapy—in other words, they use it to shock the patients. Are they still doing that? I guess I assumed shock therapy was something done in the old days of mental health treatment. But the electronic device, with its switches and dials and meters, looks relatively modern, so I guess it's still done—at least in this hospital.

I ask my guide, "Uh, will I get to observe electroconvulsive therapy as part of my job?"

She says, "Not likely."

I'm not sure if that makes me happy or not. After all, I am here to learn. But maybe there are some things I'd rather learn about from textbooks.

Outside the treatment building, standing on the sidewalk, my guide hands me a card that has a large letter "H" printed on it. She tells me all the wards in the institution are individual buildings known as "cottages," and each of them is identified by a large letter painted on the front door.

The card has two names hand-written on it, Mr. Grimm and Mrs. Grimm. My guide says they're the "houseparents" in charge of Cottage H.

Grimm? What kind of name is that? Like in the old Grimm's fairy tales?

I try not to look surprised at their odd names, but as it turns out, my guide isn't looking at me anyway; she's looking at her watch. She points farther on down the sidewalk and says, "You can find your own way to Cottage H. Introduce yourself to the cottage houseparents. In your free time, you can walk around the grounds if you want to, but don't try to visit any of the other wards or go into any of the treatment buildings on your own."

She starts to walk away, but then turns back and points toward another small brick building. "That's the staff cafeteria building. You can go there for lunch if you want to, but it's only open from twelve noon until one PM."

She hurries away, and I'm left on my own. It feels kind of odd to be left all alone in a place like this, but so far, there hasn't really been anything to be worried about.

I head down the sidewalk in the direction she'd pointed. The sidewalk runs between the brick buildings, each of them, as she said, are identified by a large letter painted on the front door. But they're not in alphabetical order. So what does the lettering refer to? The more I learn about this place, the weirder it seems.

I keep going, but so far, I haven't seen a building identified as "H." Could I have missed it? And I haven't met a single person since I began walking, so there's nobody to ask. Why aren't there any people out and about? Maybe the patients really are all locked up inside the buildings, but where are all the employees?

Finally, I see some other people coming toward me, two men and a woman. Should I ask them where Cottage H is?

I decide against it. I don't know if those people are staff or patients.

I see that all three of them, even the woman, are wearing white shirts and black pants. Is that some kind of standard way for the employees here to dress?

I make sure to maintain my pace, as if I know exactly where I'm going.

As they approach, all three of them stare at me. Do they think I'm a patient? Just to make sure they don't think that, I point to my student visitor badge.

They pass by without even acknowledging me. If they are employees, I don't understand why they weren't more friendly. I showed them my student visitor badge, didn't I? Don't they ever get student visitors here? I again have the worrying feeling that they don't like outsiders here. Why? Is everybody in this place hiding something?

As I continue on, I notice that none of the buildings are very large. My guide referred to them as "cottages," but the buildings don't look much like cottages. They're just rectangular brick buildings, and the only windows they have are small and way up high on the walls. Maybe the idea is that the patients can't escape through such small high windows.

I still haven't found a building labeled "H." I look at the card again to be sure I'm looking for the right place. Yes, it just says, "H." Again, I wonder what the letters stand for. Is it some kind of code indicating how dangerous the patients are?

My guide said Mr. and Mrs. Grimm are known as "houseparents." Why would they be called houseparents? Maybe they just don't want to call them guards.

Finally, at the very end of the sidewalk, I find Cottage H. I wonder why they assigned me to the cottage that's at the far end of the institution. Are they trying to keep me away from the main part of the hospital?

Three

I pretty much expect the large wooden front door of Cottage H to be locked, but when I turn the handle, it opens right up.

Just inside the door, a very thin, very pale, elderly man with almost no hair is sitting in a chair that's blocking my way in. Is he the door guard? I point to my "student visitor" badge.

He takes a quick glance at it, moves his chair out of my way, and begins to furiously write down notes. The only problem is, he doesn't have a pen to write with, and whatever notebook he thinks he's "writing" his notes on must be in his imagination.

I hurry on past him, Jeez. What the hell was that all about? Is he some kind of weird mental note-taking door guard?

I chuckle to myself. No reason to be nervous about him. I guess that was just my first introduction to the world of mental illness. I wonder what other kinds of odd behavior I'm going to encounter on this ward.

The first thing I notice is that there are not very many patients, and the ward is very quiet. In fact, it's totally quiet! How can that be? It's definitely not what I expected a mental ward to be like. But then, what did I expect, a raucous place with the patients running around yelling at each other? Maybe I didn't expect anything quite that bad, but totally quiet? How is that even possible?

But now I see that all the patients on this ward are old men. Are old men with mental problems always so quiet? Doesn't seem likely.

All of the old men are dressed alike, in gray sweatshirts and sweatpants. Is it some kind of patient uniform? And they're all wearing what looks like thick black socks instead of shoes. Why wouldn't they let them have shoes? Maybe whoever is running this ward demands quiet, and they don't even like the sound of shoes when the patients move around. But wait, none of the old men *are* moving around. The patients are either seated on wooden benches that are lined up along the walls of the long and somewhat narrow room, or else they're sitting in rows at the far end of the room in front of a smallish TV that's bolted to the ceiling. Are the patients forbidden to move around, along with being required to remain totally quiet? Do they have to get permission to get up and move around? How could they enforce a rule like that?

Okay, it looks like I've been assigned to an old men's ward. At least it should be safe here, a lot easier dealing with quiet old men than dealing with a ward with younger, maybe hyperactive, crazies running around chasing imaginary butterflies.

But then, on second thought, maybe this is going to turn out to be a boring experience. I still don't know if my independent study credit will mean I'll have to write some kind of report about what I learn here. If it's always this quiet and this boring, what will I have to report?

Not far from the rows of TV watchers is a middle-aged woman sitting behind a beat-up gray metal desk that looks about as old as the building itself. She seems to be sorting through a stack of papers. Is she Mrs. Grimm, the "houseparent" named on my assignment card?

When she sees me coming, she stands up. She's dressed in the same kind of outfit as those people I saw walking on the sidewalk, white shirt and black pants. I wonder if she's alone on this ward with all these old men. But she looks like she could handle them; she's not very tall, but she's stout. Quite strong looking for a woman her age.

She comes toward me, smiling with her hand held out. At least everybody in this institution isn't unfriendly. I take it as a good sign.

I shake her hand, but before I can say anything, she says, "Well, young man, you must be the psychology student."

Time to be friendly. I smile back at her. "Yes, ma'am, but I'm only an undergraduate. Third year."

She lets go of my hand, and it seems like a little bit of her smile fades at my mention of only being an undergraduate.

Maybe she thinks I'll be a burden instead of being helpful. Well, that's probably true: even though I am in my third year at the university, I've only taken the one introductory psychology class. What do I know about dealing with mental patients?

I keep on smiling as I point to my "Student Visitor" badge and say, "I'm Scott. Uh, like it says."

Her welcoming smile comes back on. "Well, it's nice to meet you, Scott. We were told you'd be visiting us today. My husband, Mr. Grimm, is in a meeting, but he'll be back soon. In the meantime, how about I walk you around and introduce you to some of our guests."

Guests? I assume she's referring to the patients, but the way she said "guests" makes me wonder if she might have a bit of a sarcastic streak in her. I say, "That would be great, ma'am."

I'm trying to make sure she can't tell how nervous I am, and so far, she seems to take my words of greeting at face value. Good. As my father always said, it's important to give a good first impression.

She leads me down the middle of the long room which she refers to as "the dayroom." She nods to each of the men we pass, but she doesn't say anything to them. They barely glance at us.

None of the old men look very happy. Maybe they're all depressed. I read somewhere that depression was becoming the national mental illness. Maybe all these old men are here because they're depressed.

As we walk through the ward, one old fellow with a full head of pure white hair makes eye contact with me. He follows me with his quick blue-gray eyes until we're completely past him.

Why did that old man stare at me when none of the others did? I'd better watch out for that one.

We walk on, and Mrs. Grimm doesn't say anything about the old man that was staring at me. Maybe she didn't notice.

We pass a doorway that leads into what looks like a dining hall with rows of tables and chairs. She notices me looking in there and says, "That's where they eat. Two light meals a day.

You can help us with that."

I'm not sure how I can help with the meals. It doesn't seem likely these old men get hard to handle at mealtime, but what do I know? Maybe they fight with each other for the food.

As we pass the ward's front door, she points at the thin old man who pretended to take notes as I entered. "I assume you met the Scribbler. He's one of our longest serving guests. Believe it or not, he's been here on this same ward for more than twenty years."

"Yes, he, uh, seemed to be pretending to take notes about me."

"Well, that's what he does." She smiles at the old man. "Don't you, Scribbler?" That sets him off furiously taking even more imaginary notes.

So she has a nickname for the pale note-taking man; he's the Scribbler. I wonder if she's given other men on the ward nicknames.

But I'd better not ask that. I'm here as a student, to learn. Therefore, my task should be to simply observe and learn. Be a fly on the wall; I bet that's the advice my father would give me. Near the end, he said, "Just keep your mouth shut and pay attention to every single thing you see and hear." After saying that, he added, "Maybe people will think you're dumb, but why open your mouth and prove it?" But then, he added he didn't think I was dumb, "only a bit shy." In fact, he told me I could accomplish anything I wanted. "If you want it enough."

The next patient we approach is a big square-shouldered man who's standing against the wall with his arms crossed in front of himself. He's the only patient on the ward who's not wearing the standard gray sweatshirt; he's wearing a short-sleeved black T-shirt, and his bulging arm muscles are larger and more defined than would seem possible in a place like this. I doubt if they have a weight room.

As we pass by him, he surprises me by growling, and my startled reaction causes Mrs. Grimm to chuckle. "Another long-termer," she says. "As you might have guessed, his nickname is the Growler. But don't worry. All he does is growl. We don't have any troublemakers on this ward."

At the end of the ward, a doorway leads to a room that contains only beds, simple narrow cots, arranged in tight rows. Mrs. Grimm says, "And this is where they sleep. Obviously."

The beds are so close together, it makes me wonder what keeps them from killing each other in the night. But maybe what Mrs. Grimm said is true; maybe there really aren't any troublemakers on this ward. I hope not. Even though I'm presenting myself as a third-year psychology student from the university, it reminds me once again that I actually don't have a clue about how I might deal with a troublesome mental patient.

Next, Mrs. Grimm leads me down a short, but wide, hallway where we pass a rather large black man with graying hair who's pacing back and forth. He's the first one of the patients I've seen actually moving. As we get closer to him, I can hear him mumbling as he walks back and forth on a tight path. His mumbling contains a string of cuss words that are apparently angry verbal attacks on some "Goddam bitch."

The man is so large and so angry sounding, I wonder if I've finally met my first dangerous patient. I'm still determined to simply observe and learn, but my curiosity overcomes my resistance, so I ask Mrs. Grimm who that angry man is.

"Oh him," she says. "That's the Cusser. You don't need to worry about him. He may act angry, but he's not mad at anybody except his wife. He's another one of our long-term guests. Been here since about forever, but he's still angry at his wife for putting him in here. We keep him here in this back hallway so he can cuss out his wife as much as he wants to, as long as he keeps it low."

She leads me on down that hallway until we arrive at what is obviously the ward restroom. It's a narrow but fairly long room, with one whole wall lined with sinks and old-fashioned tall urinals. The opposite wall is lined with ancient-looking yellowed toilets. There are no dividers between the urinals and no stalls around the toilets, so if any of the patients are shy about others watching them do their business, this is obviously the wrong place for them.

There's one old man sitting on one of the toilets. He seems to be straining, and if he notices us looking at him, he doesn't let on.

Mrs. Grimm doesn't pay any attention to him, so I guess the male patients on this ward don't mind her coming in while they're using the facilities. She points in the general direction of the urinals. "Notice how clean everything is. On this ward, we've taught our guests how to clean up after themselves."

She's right: the entire restroom is quite clean, maybe even cleaner than the restrooms at the university.

Mrs. Grimm leads me back into the ward, and as we enter the dayroom, she points at a tall, dark-haired man who's just come in through the ward's front door. "Oh, here's my husband," she says.

He's wearing the same white shirt and black pants that seems to be the employee uniform in this institution. She seems happy to see him. Maybe she doesn't like being alone on the ward without him, surrounded by a lot of male mental patients.

Mrs. Grimm leads me to her husband and introduces him as "Mr. Grimm." She lightly touches my shoulder and says, "This is the student they said would be visiting us. His name is Scott."

I stick out my hand, but he ignores it. And he's not smiling. Doesn't he like the idea of a student coming onto his ward?

"Come with me," he says in a gruff voice. "I'll go over the ward rules with you."

Walking fast, he leads me to a door behind his wife's desk. He goes through the door, and although he doesn't say anything, I assume I'm supposed to follow him. He leads me into what I expect to be an office, but it's not; it's a small room with only a bed, a dresser, and a TV set. It must mean that they live right here on the ward. That must be why they call them "houseparents." Does that mean no other employees ever come onto this ward? Do the two of them run it all by themselves? What do they do at night when the patients go to bed? Do they take turns staying up to watch them? I can't even start to imagine what it would be like to live full time inside a ward full of mental patients.

I follow Mr. Grimm through that room and into another small room that must be his office. It's startling plain, with no pictures on the walls and no personal items of any kind. There's a battered metal gray desk, two chairs, and a gray metal filing cabinet.

Mr. Grimm sits down behind the desk and points to the chair that's in front of the desk.

I try to think what to say to him, but there's no need, because before I'm even seated, he says, "Fourteen men, all of them old, as I'm sure you noticed. However, you may have noticed that some of them look a bit younger. It's because of the powerful emotion-killing drugs they've been on for so many years. Keeps them from forming facial wrinkles."

He's been talking fast, but now he pauses for a moment, as if he's giving me time to take all that in before he goes on. "Some people at this institution call this the 'permanent' ward because the men here have no money and no relatives willing to take them in. As a result, they're likely to live out their days without ever setting foot outside this ward. But here, we don't call it that. You should refer to it simply as Cottage H. Everyone will know which ward you're referring to. Any questions?"

Actually, I have a lot of questions, like why is it so quiet on this ward and why is nobody moving around. But maybe I'd better not ask him about that. He might take it as criticism. I just say, "No, sir. I understand."

"Good. Now, your badge identifies you as a student visitor. Make sure you wear it at all times, and be careful not to cover it up with a jacket or anything like that."

I wonder if any of the old men on this ward would really think someone as young as me would be a patient on their ward.

Mr. Grimm seems to anticipate my question. "Without your ID, because of your youth, some of the patients might think you're a staff member. If they start talking to you about their troubles, or start complaining about their medications, just point to your badge and inform them that you are only a student visitor. Understand?"

Actually, I'm not sure I do understand why he's making such a big deal about always identifying myself as a student, but I just say, "Yes, sir."

He stares at me for a moment, and then says, "This is an open ward, and most of them are voluntary patients. That means they can go outside if they want to. But few of them ever do. Nevertheless, if they demand to go outside, tell them to come talk to me."

If this is an open ward, and they are voluntary patients, why would they have to get permission from him to go outside? I know the front door is unlocked, so if any of the patients decided to go outside, who's going to stop them? The Scribbler, the frail-looking imaginary-note-taking man who's posted inside the ward's front door? He seems to act like a door guard, but it's not likely he could stop any one of the men on this ward if they really wanted to get past him.

I decide this is not the time to get inquisitive. If I'm going to spend my student time on this ward, I'm sure all my questions will be answered in due time. No reason to say anything that might be interpreted as questioning his judgment. I just keep on smiling and nodding.

"That's about it," he says. "Ready to get going?"

"Sure. Uh, what am I supposed to do, exactly? Just walk around and watch the patients?"

Now it's his turn to nod. "Yes. For now, just do that. Watch and learn. Later on, we'll find some things for you to do. Nothing much, just this and that. But you're here mostly as a student. To learn."

"Okay," I say. "Uh, can I ask, are you a mental health prac-titioner? I mean are you a . . . psychologist or . . . ?"

"Me? No. I've been through some training programs, but that was a long time ago. My title is Senior Aide. Same for my wife, Mrs. Grimm. Any more questions?"

I have a lot more questions, but he seems kind of impatient, so I decide to hold off on asking them. I should just try to find out more by doing what he said, observing the patients.

He takes some papers out of his desk drawer and looks at them, so I assume that means the interview is over. I thank him and quietly leave the office.

As I pass Mrs. Grimm, who is back sitting at her observation desk, she smiles at me and says, "All set?"

"I guess so. Maybe I'll just walk around and . . . uh, observe."

"Good. If you have any questions, just come ask me. I'll be right here. I'm always right here. Been here for . . . well, let's see. More than twenty years now. Isn't that something?"

She's been here on this ward for more than twenty years? That's more years than I've been alive? It's hard for me to get my head around the idea of a person staying in one place doing the same thing for so many years, but I don't say that; I just smile and nod and move on out into the ward.

I stroll through the dayroom, very aware that the sound of my shoes on the wooden floor is making the only noise in the place. I try to walk quieter, but it's impossible. You'd think me making the only noise would cause the old men to look up at me as I pass by them, but they don't. It's like they don't even know I'm here. Spooky.

I continue to walk and observing. But there's not much to observe. Actually, I'm not exactly sure what I'm supposed to be looking for. Not only is it boring, but I'm also worried that when I get back to the university they might have me write a report on what I'm learning here. But nothing is happening on this ward, so what would I have to report?

Four

I'm still thinking about what kind of report I might have to write about this "non-experience," when the white-haired man that made eye contact with me earlier waves me over. His pure white hair tells he must be pretty old, but just as Mr. Grimm had predicted, his face lacks any deep wrinkles, so he looks younger. And unlike any of the other sad-looking patients on this "permanent" ward, he has an odd smile on his face. Actually, it's not what you'd call a real smile—more of a sly smirk.

Why is he calling me over? I hesitate before I respond. Neither of the Grimms has actually told me not to talk to the patients, but they did say I was just supposed to observe. I go a little closer to him and point to my badge to make sure he knows I'm not a member of the staff.

He nods to show me he understands, then he moves a bit to the side of the wooden bench he's sitting on and pats it to indicate that I should sit down next to him. I'm not sure I should do that. He seems harmless enough, and Mrs. Grimm did say none of the old men on the ward were troublemakers. But still, what do I know about how to deal with a mental patient? Maybe I should just continue doing what I've been doing, walking and observing, no matter how boring it is. But he's just a white-haired old man, and he's acting very friendly. He seems to urgently want me to sit next to him. Maybe he's just lonely. Mr. Grimm said the old men on this ward don't have any relatives to take care of them. That probably means they don't get any visitors. The old men in my father's dying facility never got any visitors, and it always made me feel sorry for them. This old guy probably just sees me as somebody new to talk to, so there shouldn't be anything wrong with just sitting with him for a few minutes. Besides, it has to be better than just walking around being bored.

I look around to make sure nobody is watching me. Mrs. Grimm is still at her desk reading something, and all of the other patients are either over at the end of the room watching TV, or they're just sitting quietly, apparently involved inside their own thoughts, so I sit down next to him.

The old man grabs my arm and pulls me closer. "Listen to me, young man," he whispers, "I have to tell you a secret. Before it is too late."

I barely manage to keep from jerking my arm free and running away from him, but I know there's no reason to be afraid of this old man. Besides, I'm curious about what he said. A secret? Before it's too late? Too late for what? I'm not sure how I'm supposed to react, so I just say, "Okay."

Apparently, that's enough for him. He leans closer and whispers, "If I tell you my secret, you must not tell anyone else."

I'm careful not to let my face give away anything. I think he really wants to tell me his secret, so even if I don't say anything, I'm pretty sure he'll keep on talking. Maybe this old man will give me something to report back to the university after all.

"What I need to tell you, young man, is about a trick I played on my mean neighbor lady. Her name was Steinberg. That name alone should tell you what kind of person she was. Should I tell you what I did to her?"

I'm pretty sure Steinberg is a Jewish name. And this old man's got some kind of foreign accent? Could he be a German? If he really is from Germany, he could be old enough to have been in the war. Is he a German who hates Jews? Maybe I'd better not get involved in whatever it is he wants. Maybe I should just tell him I've got something else to do.

But I don't actually have anything else to do except walk around the ward being bored, and besides, if I tell him I'm busy and move on, it might get him all upset. I don't want my first encounter on a mental ward to be getting one of the patients upset, so I'd better just continue with my smiling and nodding approach.

He says, "The whole incident started with my dog. His name was Adolph. The police came to my house and said they had received a complaint about my dog making too much noise.

They said the complaint came from my neighbor lady, Mrs. Steinberg, and that she said I had thrown a rock at her. She told the police I was trying to hurt her. That was a compete untruth. I had thrown a rock, but it was only a little rock, and it was thrown only to scare her. If I would have wanted to hit her with that rock, I would have. Let me tell you, young man, I used to have quite a good throwing arm, when I was younger. I played games with balls many times. I told the policeman that. I told him I was only trying to scare her back inside her house to get her to mind her own business. I knew the real reason fat ugly Mrs. Steinberg was angry was because my dog had been defecating on her precious lawn. I had been watching her out my window for some time, and I knew she had a relationship with the lawn man she had hired to keep her little green lawn trimmed down nice and neat. And she had put silly little flowers all along the edges of her front side-walk. In my opinion, it was a foolish waste of money in our old run-down neighborhood."

The old man stops talking and stares at me for a long moment.

What does that look mean? Does he want some kind of response from me? The way he's looking at me makes me uncomfortable. I'm kind of interested in his story, but aren't I supposed to be just observing, like a fly on the wall? But of course, I'm not really a fly on the wall. The old man sees me simply as a fellow human being, and he wants to tell me a story. No harm in listening. Even a fly on the wall can listen, right?

The old man says, "Do you not believe me?"

A dilemma. Should I say I do believe him, or should I try to think of something more noncommittal to say? I'm not sure I should be encouraging a mental patient to tell stories that involve the police. But even though he is a patient on this ward, he's not acting very crazy, at least not as crazy as crazy people in the movies do. I decide a minimal response can't hurt, so I just shrug. Nothing more noncommittal than a shrug.

"She was very foolish about her precious little lawn, and that was the real reason she had called the police. And here they were, seeming to take her nonsense seriously. What do you think of that?"

I go with the shrug response again.

"The crazy woman was yelling very loud at the police demanding that they should take my poor old dog Adolph away. She said she was going to file charges against me. The police must have seen how crazy she was, but they said they would have to take the dog to the city pound until the dispute was resolved. So, what do you think I did, son?"

I try the shrug routine again, but this time it doesn't work. He's staring at me, apparently wanting me to answer his question. If I want to hear the rest of his story, I guess I have to say some-thing. "Uh, I suspect there was nothing you could do."

"That is correct. They took my poor dog Adolph away, and I couldn't do a thing about it." He looks around as if to see if anyone else is listening.

I wonder why he did that. Is he worried that his talking to me is making too much noise on this weirdly-quiet ward? Maybe he's afraid Mrs. Grimm is going to come and make him stop telling me his story. But he has been whispering. From where she is, I don't think she can hear us. I again worry that maybe I'm not supposed to be talking to the patients.

I'm thinking I should get up and go back to just "observ-ing" when he again leans close to me and whispers, "Listen, son, I will now let you in on a little secret. I actually let the police take Adolph away without an argument from me because I had decided to resolve the situation myself. Do you know what my plan was?"

The shrug response seemed to work before, so I stick with it.

The old man laughs a short laugh. "Well, of course you don't know. Nobody could know what I had up my sleeve. Do you know what that means, young man, to have a trick up your sleeve?"

I'm starting to wonder if this old man is just having a bit of fun with me. He might be a person who likes to make up stories.

In fact, he may tell this same story to every new person who walks onto the ward. Still, I have to admit I am a bit curious about where he's going with his weird story. And there was that thing he said about having to tell somebody before it was too late. I say, "Yes, I get it. Having a secret strategy."

"Exactly right. I knew you would understand. That's why I picked you, young man. You're smart. I can tell the smart ones. I will now tell you what it was I had up my sleeve. First, I had to wait until she came out of her house to chase away some children that had dared to step on her precious lawn, and then I ran right over to her and started yelling, pretending to be very angry that she had got the police to take my dog Adolph away. She said it was my own fault. She said I should have controlled the mutt. I asked her what I was going to do now because I didn't have the money to go get poor Adolph out of the dog pound. I told her if only she would have left him alone long enough for Adolph to tell me next week's lottery numbers, I would have had enough money to build a fence to keep him off of her stupid lawn.

Again, the old man stops talking. It's as if he needs me to keep responding. I have to admit he does have me curious. Does he really believe his dog can talk and tell him lottery numbers? He's a mental patient, so maybe he believes all kinds of strange things. But I don't want to ask him if he believes dogs can talk. I don't know if it's a good thing or a bad thing to make dismissive comments about a mental patient saying crazy things.

I'm still trying to decide what to do, when he says, "Now, young man, guess what mean old Mrs. Steinberg did? I will tell you what she did. She laughed right in my face. Called me a crazy old German. She said I was totally crazy to think a dog could talk, let alone know the correct lottery numbers. 'No, no,' I told her, 'the dog really does know the winning numbers. and he always gets them right every time, almost.' She laughed at me again and said, 'Well if your stupid dog can tell you the correct lottery numbers, why don't you have any money?' I told her, 'Yes, Adolph does know the correct numbers, but when he tells them to me, and I bet on them, the real numbers always turn out to be either one number higher or one number lower.' At that point, Mrs. Steinberg called me stupid. Said if I had half a brain in my head, I would have picked all the numbers higher or lower than what the dog told me. So you see, young man, her response told me I had her. She was responding just like I hoped she would. So, what do you think I did next?"

I'm pretty sure by now the old man wants to keep on telling me his story. His questions are only to make sure I stick with him. Maybe that's all he wanted in the first place. Maybe this weird storytelling is just a way to get himself some attention. In fact, maybe that's what his mental condition is, a need to be the center of attention. If that's what this old man's mental condition is, I may have something interesting to report after all. I again use the shrug response to keep him going.

"I will now tell you what I did next, young man. What I did was act very surprised. Like this." The old man opens his mouth and throws up his arms in a mock display of acting very surprised. "'By damn,' I said to her, 'why didn't I think of that?' I acted real grateful and told her that as soon as I got my disability check, I would go right down to the pound and pay to get my poor dog out so I could pick all the numbers just above and below whatever numbers my dog told me. And now, young man, I'll tell what happened next. It was exactly what I knew was going to happen. Mrs. Steinberg went to the dog pound and paid to get my dog for herself. I could just imagine her over there in her house trying to get the dog to tell her the lottery numbers. I knew all I had to do was wait for the chance to put the rest of my plan into action. And sure enough, it wasn't long before she let the dog out to poop. She sent him over to poop in the dirt of my yard of course, not on her precious green lawn. I grabbed a pencil and piece of paper and hurried outside. I kneeled down in front of the dog. Of course, my old dog Adolph was happy to see me. He nuzzled my face. Do you know what that means, young man? Nuzzled? Here, let me show you." He slips off of the bench and kneels in front of me. "Come down here on the floor with me. You be me, and I'll be the dog. I'll show you how it worked."

It's the first time he's asked me to actually participate in his story, and I'm not sure how I should respond. What would the other patients think if they saw us down on our knees in front of each other? They'd probably think I was as crazy as he is. Even more important, what would Mrs. Grimm think if she happened to look up from whatever she's reading and saw me down on the floor, face to face with this old man? I'm interested to see where the old man is going with his story, but I know I can't do what he's asking me to do.

He seems to quickly realize I'm not going to get down on the floor with him, so finally, with some effort, he gets up and re-seats himself on the bench. "Okay," he says, "I'll just tell you how it went instead of showing you. Every time the dog nuzzled my face, I nodded as if he'd told me something, and then I wrote down a number on my piece of paper. Do you get it?"

I nod. "You were pretending the dog was talking to you, telling you the lottery numbers."

"That is it! Exactly. I knew you were a smart young fellow. And as you have probably guessed already, Mrs. Steinberg was watching me from behind the frilly curtains of her living room window. Pretty soon, she came out and grabbed the dog by its collar. She dragged it back into her house and slammed the door. You can probably imagine what was going through her head."

By now, I know all I have to do is smile and keep paying attention to him, and he will continue telling me the story.

"I will tell you what she was doing. She was over there in her house trying to figure out why the dog told me the lottery numbers and not her. Now, I will tell you what I did next. As soon as my disability check arrived in the mail, I hurried right down to the bank and cashed it. I had them give it all to me in small bills." He stops talking again and winks at me. "Get it?"

This time, I'm not exactly sure where he is going with his story, but I suspect it meant he was hatching a plan to make his neighbor lady think he'd won the lottery. I nod again.

"I knew you would figure it out. The moment I saw you walk onto this ward, I could tell you were one of the smart ones.

There aren't many of us in this world, are there?" He winks at me.

I just smile to keep him going.

"Well, young man, on lottery night, I waited until the TV announced the winning numbers, and then I put my disability money into my pocket and ran out my front door. I stood in my front yard yelling and dancing and waving some of my old lottery tickets around. As soon as I saw old Mrs. Steinberg looking out of her window, I ran off down the street, So, why do you think I did that?"

"You were pretending you'd won."

"Right you are, my boy, right you are. I waited around the corner for a bit, and then I came back and started yelling loud enough to be sure she could hear me. 'Ha ha, look at me,' I yelled. 'I'm rich and you're not.' I tossed some of my disability money up into the air, and then I danced around it until she came out onto her front porch. She just stood there staring at me, her hands on her hips. I fanned out all of my disability money and yelled at her, 'Ha ha, the jokes on you. You may have my dog, but I'm the one he tells the numbers to, not you. He's loyal to me.' Well, let me tell you, young man, it was obvious I had made her angry. Really angry. She went back inside her house, but soon she came right back out. And guess what she had in her hand?"

I do my usual shrug.

"She had a knife. A great big butcher knife. She came charging across her lawn toward me. I picked up my money as fast as I could and ran for my front door. But she was faster than she looked. I made it inside my house, but she forced her way in and put that big knife up against my throat. 'It's my dog now,' she screamed. 'So that money is mine. Hand it over, or I will slit your damn throat. I swear I will.'" The old man leaned even closer to me and whispered, "Well, young man, as I'm sure you will agree, I had to do it to protect myself, did I not? I took that big knife away from her and stuck it right in her fat gut. What do you think of that? It was self defense, was it not?"

Looking at the frail old man, I'm not sure he would have been strong enough to easily get a knife away from a woman he'd been describing as big and fat. I'm beginning to suspect he's making the whole thing up and isn't bothering with all the details. Nevertheless, I try to keep a straight face as I say, "You stabbed her? Really?"

"I sure did. Did her in good. What choice did I have? It was either her or me. But after I did it, I didn't know what I was supposed to do. The police had been there only a few days before, and they would surely remember she said I was threatening her. I stood there in my front hallway, looking down at her dead body with that big knife sticking straight out of her gut. Now, guess what happened next?"

Once again, I try not to let my facial response give anything away, but I'm starting to wonder if what he's telling me could possibly be true. Could this old man really have killed someone? No, I push that thought away. More likely, he's just a weird old guy who likes to make up crazy stories. In the movies, they portray crazy people as making up strange things, like believing they're secretly being spied on by the CIA or something like that. I guess when I came here, I suspected I'd see some weird behavior, but nothing had prepared me for this kind of situation.

Only a few minutes on this ward, and I've already got myself involved in something I don't know how to deal with. Maybe I should have been more careful. On the other hand, maybe this old man is just some kind of storyteller. He probably tells his horrific stories to anybody who'll listen. He probably didn't really kill his neighbor. On the other hand, he *is* a patient in a mental hospital. Was he committed to this institution after being convicted of killing somebody? Either way, I know I have to report what this old man is telling me. I should go tell Mrs. Grimm right away and ask her if the old man likes to make up stories. Hopefully, she already knows the story about him killing his neighbor is fake, and she'll tell me not to worry about it.

The old man must realize I'm about to get up and leave, because he grabs ahold of my sleeve. "Wait a minute, young man, that is not the end of the story. Not by a long way. What happened next was that my dog Adolph came in through the front door which was still standing open. I hurried to close the door, and by the time I turned back around, the dog was right next to her body, lapping up her blood off of the floor. The way he eagerly lapped at the blood made me think poor Adolph was really hungry. Maybe after she had retrieved Adolph from out of the dog pound, she had never bothered to buy dog food for him. But it gave me an idea. As a test, I pulled the butcher knife out of her gut and used it to hack off a little piece of her leg. I put that piece of her into Adolph's dish, and sure enough, he ran over and ate it right up. I'll tell you what that taught me, young man, to a dog, we humans are just walking meat. Once we're dead, we are like any other dog food. Maybe even more tasty."

He stops talking and this time I know he isn't going to go on unless I say something.

I don't want to be rude to the old man, but what can I say about his weird story? I'd better not say I don't believe him. He might react badly if I do that. I sure wish I knew more about how to deal with mental patients. After all, I've only taken one beginning psychology course, and they sure didn't tell me anything about how to deal with a situation like this.

I decide the best course of action, for the moment, is to act like I do believe him. I say, "Well, that's quite a story, sir. What did the police say?"

"The police? Naw. They never found out. I hacked the old bitch woman all up and put her in the freezer. I fed bits of her to my dog every day until she was all gone."

He cut the woman into pieces and fed her to his dog. Is that actually possible?

"Uh, and nobody missed her?"

"Not for quite a while. Her son, who I guess lived up in Alaska or somewhere, did not show up for months and months. When he finally came to see her, he did report her missing. But by the time the cops came to talk to me about it, she had been entirely eaten by my good old dog Adolph. In fact, he was eating up the last of her even as the police stood there at my front door talking to me. And let me tell you, that was one fat and happy dog."

Five

I thank the old man for telling me his story, and then I get up and head straight for Mrs. Grimm. Whether the story is true or not, I know I should tell her what the old man had told me.

After I lay the story out for her, including the part where he said he chopped up his neighbor lady and fed her to his dog, she does seem a bit disturbed by it. She asks me to point out which one of the patients had told me such a gruesome story.

I point. "That white-haired guy. Over there. On that bench."

She barely glances at him, which makes me wonder if she already suspected which patient it was. "Oh, him," she says. "Mr. Eichner. He hasn't been here very long. At least not this time. When he came back a few months ago, he kept wanting to leave. But he's calmed down now. Like I said, we don't have any troublemakers on our ward." She glances at Eichner again. "At least not usually."

The way she paused before saying "not usually" might mean there had been trouble on this ward in the past. Do they now have a special way to deal with troublesome patients? They do seem to have figured out some way of keeping them all quiet. Or maybe they just get rid of the troublemakers. I say, "But what if his story is true? Should we report it to the police or . . . something?"

"The police?" She shakes her head. "No. You can't take anything these patients say as real. Sometimes, they . . . make things up."

"Oh, so this Mister Eichner likes to make up stories?"

"Well . . ." She turns and looks back at the door to their apartment. "Actually, I think you should talk to Mr. Grimm about this."

"Really? I should bother him? Can't you tell him about it?"

"Well, he might have questions. Go ahead and knock on his door."

I go to his door, but I hesitate. I was supposed to just observe. I shouldn't have even let that old man tell me such a gruesome story. Now what? Am I in trouble? Even worse, maybe I'm going to get one of the patients in trouble, and on my first day on the ward. Maybe it would have been better to just not tell Mrs. Grimm about the old man's story. After all, he did ask me not to tell anybody else.

Mrs. Grimm is looking at me. "Go ahead," she says. "Just knock."

I rap lightly on the door.

At first, I'm not sure he's going to answer, which would be okay with me, but I know he's in there because I hear some drawers being slammed shut. Then, I hear him say, "Come in."

I go into their apartment and find him waiting in the doorway to his office. "Oh, it's you, Scott. Come on in."

We go into his office, and he sits behind his desk He pushes aside some official-looking papers and gestures for me to sit down.

I sit down and tell him the story Mr. Eichner told me, emphasizing that I hadn't done anything to encourage it. "In fact, I don't know why he picked me to talk to. I was just walking past him, and he waved me over. I didn't think there was anything wrong with just listening to him for a few minutes."

"No, no, you didn't do anything wrong, Scott." He looks down at his desk for a few moments before he adds, "Well, I wouldn't worry about it. Some of them just like to make up strange stories."

I quickly say, "That's what I thought. At first. But he seemed sort of . . . urgent. He said he had to tell the story to someone before it was too late."

Mr. Grimm nods thoughtfully. "So Eichner is back to thinking he's going to die, is he? I don't know where he's getting that idea. He kept on telling us he didn't have much time left. We had the doctor look him over. They even did some blood tests, but they said he was fine. True, he's getting pretty old, but there's no reason to think he's going to die anytime soon."

"Uh, right. He didn't say anything about dying. And he doesn't seem sick or anything."

"No, he's not ill. At least as far as we know." Mr. Grimm leans forward and puts his elbows on the desk. He stares right into my eyes. "Listen, young man, you have to take a lot of what these patients tell you with a grain of salt. They may be old, but some of them still have a few tricks up their sleeves." He leans back in his chair.

It's interesting that he used the exact same expression that Eichner did about having tricks up his sleeve. I never mentioned that when I told him the story.

Mr. Grimm is obviously waiting for me to say something, but I don't know what he wants me to say. He's the person in charge of this ward, so he should know what kind of person Eichner is, but he's not coming right out to say the old man was lying to me. In fact, he seems a bit . . . I don't know, maybe troubled at what I told him. But I have the feeling he's trying not to show any reaction. I know I should just stop talking, but I don't want to be impolite on my first day. Besides, I need to know what I'm supposed to do if Eichner tries to talk to me again. I say, "All right. I understand that maybe it was just a story he made up, but what do we know about him? Maybe we should go to the place he lived and ask around. If he did kill his neighbor—"

Mr. Grimm shakes his head "No, we don't want to do that. We don't know anything about our patients' backgrounds, and its better that way. Here at Cottage H, we take these men as they are."

"But do you think there's any possibility his story might be true? He made the story sound so real."

"Do I believe he killed his neighbor lady and fed her to his dog?" Mr. Grimm waves his hand as if he's shooing the idea away. "No. Eichner does have something of a checkered past, but we haven't heard of anything like that. However, since you're going to be working with us here for a few months, I might as well tell you more about this ward. First off, some of the old men here have been housed in this same building for a very long time.

More than twenty years, some of them."

"Yes, Mrs. Grimm introduced me to a few of the old timers. She said they had unusual nicknames."

"Oh that. Well, they were given those names a long time ago. Before my time, actually. I believe some of the nicknames go all the way back to when Eichner was on this ward in the old days."

"He was here before? And then left?"

"Yes. Apparently, back then, he was a known troublemaker. But for some reason, he got released. Or just left. Anyhow, it was all before my time. But now he's come back to us, and he hasn't caused us any trouble. At least not until now."

"So you don't think he's a . . . uh, a criminal, or something like that?"

Mr. Grimm does a false laugh and again pushes the idea away with another wave of his hand. "If he was here because of some serious crime, I would have been informed. And he wouldn't be on this ward anyhow. He'd be on a locked ward for violent patients. I'm not exactly sure what brought him back to this institution, but he's been here with us for several months now, and like I said, until now he hasn't caused us any trouble."

Mr. Grimm's words and his attitude have me worried that maybe I've gotten Mr. Eichner in trouble. I quickly say, "Actually, he was very polite in the way he told me the story. I don't think he was trying to cause any trouble."

"Be that as it may, I think we'd better keep an eye on him for a while. Let me know if he tries to tell you any more strange stories like that."

"Okay. But I'm sure he didn't mean any harm. Actually, he seemed to enjoy telling me that story. And it *was* kind of funny. I mean about the dog being able to tell winning lottery numbers."

Mr. Grimm nods, looking serious. "Well, thank you for informing me. You did well."

I'm not so sure I did well, reporting on a patient on my first day on the ward. If it gets out that I ran straight to the houseparents as soon as somebody talked to me, maybe now none of the other old men on the ward will ever talk to me. They might think of me as a tattletale. But I had to report such a horrific story, didn't I?

"Anyhow," says Mr. Grimm, moving some papers to the center of his desk. "If you'll excuse me, I have some paperwork I have to get caught up on."

I jump to my feet. "Oh, sure. I'll just go back to walking around the ward, and, uh, observing."

As I leave the office and pass by Mrs. Grimm, she says, "Everything all right?"

"Oh, sure. I just told your husband the old man's story."

"Good," she says. "Don't be afraid to tell us anything you see. And if you have any questions, don't hesitate to bring them to me. We want you to enjoy your time here with us."

I thank her and start to walk away, but she calls me back. "By the way, Scott, it's almost noon. If you want to have lunch, the staff cafeteria is only open from twelve to one. Do you know where it is?"

I tell her I do and head for the front door. When I get to the Scribbler, he moves his chair out of my way, and it sets him off on another frenzy of imaginary note-taking.

The first time the Scribbler made imaginary notes about me, I thought it was funny. Now, for some reason, it worries me. I can't exactly say why. It's like he thinks he actually is the front door guard, and he has to keep track of anybody who passes his station.

Outside, I breathe a bit easier, glad to be out of that dark ward and into the bright sunshine. I'm not all that hungry, but I do need some time to think about the old man's story and whether I did the right thing by reporting it to Mr. and Mrs. Grimm. Besides, I skipped breakfast this morning, so I probably should get something in my stomach. I head for the staff cafeteria building.

Six

Apparently, the employee cafeteria isn't open yet. There's a bunch of employees outside waiting, so I join in at the end of the line.

As I wait, I watch the employees. They're chatting among themselves, and no one speaks to me.

The only employee in the line I recognize is the very large man I'd seen earlier. He was the one teaching the teenaged patients. He's at the head of the line. He's not talking to anyone, and the moment they open the door, he rushes in.

Once we're all inside, the line moves fairly quickly to the cafeteria's food area. It's a typical self-service cafeteria type situation, like back in high school. Chrome rails to slide your tray along as you select the food you want to eat.

As I wait to get to the food area, I watch the other employees pick out their food. Especially interesting is the huge school-teacher who was first in line. He seems to have developed a masterful plan for stacking as much food as possible on the one medium-sized plate they provide. He skillfully layers the food, using a sort of architectural-looking construction made up of layers of meat interlaid with slices of cheese that could represent the floors of his food skyscraper. In between those layers, he scoops in a lot of Jello and potato salad, and then he uses leaves of lettuce to wrap around and under to keep it all from collapsing.

I'm quite impressed to see how much food can possibly be stacked onto one plate. It must have taken a lot of practice to perfect his food-stacking technique.

Once he's managed to complete his massive food construction, he pushes his tray to the desert section where he carefully picks out the largest available piece of cake before quickly pushing his tray to the end so the cashier can punch his card, which must represent some kind of discount food program for employees. Then, he hurries to a table in the far back corner and begins shoving all that food into his mouth. He must prefer to sit alone back there so no one can interrupt his eating. He's obviously an odd duck, but none of the other employees are paying any attention to him; I guess they must be used to his huge size and his wildly excessive eating habits.

When I finally get to the food area, I grab a tray and a plate and start selecting a small amount of food. The line is moving slowly, and I still haven't made it to the desert area when I realize the big schoolteacher is right behind me. Somehow, he's manages to eat all that food he stacked on his plate before I've even finished getting my food. He's filling up his plate again, using his same careful food-stacking method. Being last in line, I end up right next to him, so I get to see, close up, his food construction technique. How he manages to stack so much food onto one plate is actually quite an impressive feat.

He notices me staring at his food-building method, and he laughs at himself. "As you can see, I like to eat. And the stingy so-and-sos here only let me refill my plate once, so I have to get my first plateful taken care of fast. Now, I can relax and have conversations like anybody else while I eat my second plateful."

I finish preparing my own modest plate of food and move to the cashier where I learn it's only going to cost me a few bucks.

I'm looking around the room for a place to sit when the big schoolteacher nudges my arm and nods toward an empty table. "Let's sit over there. You're new here, aren't you?"

"Yes. It's my first day." I notice most of the other employees are sitting in small groups. Maybe I should join one of those groups so I can get to know some people here. But I don't want to be impolite to the schoolteacher. I can get to know some of the other employees later.

After the schoolteacher gets seated, and I sit across the table from him, he leans forward to read my badge. "Oh," he says between mouthfuls of food. "You're only a student." And then he laughs at himself again. "I shouldn't have said only. What I meant to say was, hey nice to see a student here for a change. You studying to be a shrink?"

"Well, I am studying psychology. But I'm only an under-graduate."

"A psych major, eh? Good for you." For some reason, he laughs again.

He certainly is a jolly fellow. Even when he isn't laughing, his eyes are. He seems like a nice person, despite his excessive eating habits.

"Me," he says, "I was only an education major. Got a degree and a teaching certificate, but no school would hire me. Cause of my size. Bad influence on the kids, they said. So I end up at this place. Can you believe it? A school teacher in a nut house? But I like the kids, and even though the pay is crap, I can eat a ton of food for only a few bucks a month." He nods toward his plate. "Even though they're only open for lunch, eating this much food in a real restaurant every day would put me in the poor house. Ha!" He goes back to shoveling food into his mouth.

I'm trying to think how to respond to that when he adds, "So, you're probably wondering how much I weigh. Well, to tell you the truth, I don't know. Somewhere north of four hundred, I 'spose. Haven't been weighed since the last time I saw the doctor. He's here from Puerto Rico. Yeah, a foreigner, like all the doctors in this place. They do their residency here in order to get a license to practice in this country. They may not know much about men-tal illness, but I ask you, would any real doctor want to work in a place like this? That Puerto Rican doctor that checked me out says I'm going to kill myself eating so much. Hell, he's probably right. But what can I say? I like to eat." He laughs again, and goes back to eating his food so fast I have to consciously slow my own eating down in order not to get caught up in his eating and talking rhythm.

"So," he says, "you're here to learn about nuts, eh? How long you gonna be here?"

"Just this one semester."

"A whole semester? Great. We can eat lunch together every day. Assuming you don't mind my terrible eating habits, that is.

But I can tell you're a tolerant person. Otherwise you wouldn't have agreed to sit here and watch me eat in the first place. So, what have you learned about these nuts so far? How does being in this kind of place make you feel? Me? At first it made me feel a bit nutty too, but you get over it."

I know I'd better make my mind up quick about whether to reinforce him for believing I'll eat lunch with him every day. He's already making plans to spend time with me, and although he does seem to be a pleasant person, nobody else is joining us. The other employees probably avoid him, so if I eat lunch with him every day, I might not get to meet any of the other staff.

"Well?" he says, "why so quiet? Are you thinking about my question? When I first got here, I was afraid to talk to the patients. I didn't know *how* to talk to them. Are you feeling that way too?"

His earnest way of asking questions about who I am makes me realize I'm not used to people asking me to talk, at least not about myself. Not that I'm a shy person or anything like that, but I usually just ask people about themselves. That's usually enough to get them going, so I don't have to talk about myself.

I realize I still haven't answered his question, so I quickly say, "Well, no, not really. As a student visitor, I'm just supposed to observe and learn. It's not like I'm doing a real job here. I'm just getting three hours of class credit. Independent study, they call it."

"Right, right, but you must be a little nervous being around so many crazies. I know I was. It takes a while, but eventually you get used to 'em and realize they're just people. Maybe they're a little off in the head, but I haven't met any of 'em I couldn't talk to. I usually just make jokes about my weight. That loosens 'em up, even the real nut cases. Maybe they think I've got problems just like they do." He laughs again and sticks out his surprisingly small hand. "By the way, my name's Fred. Also known as Fat Freddy. That's what everybody calls me."

"Oh, okay. But I think I'll just call you Fred." I shake his hand. "I'm Scott."

"Pleased ta meet ya, Scott. But don't worry about the Fat Freddy thing if you hear it. I don't mind. I am fat. No doubt about that." He grins at me and goes back to eating.

He stops eating and laughs again. "Now see there. You did it again. Found a way to avoid answering my questions. Don't like talkin' about yourself? Is that it?"

"Uh, no," I say quickly. "I don't mind talking about myself. But there isn't much to tell. Like I said, I'm just a student."

"Hey, you can talk about yourself or don't. Don't matter to me one way or the other. Me, I like to talk. Once I get my belly full, that is. Okay, Scott, how about this question. Any interesting encounters so far in this place?"

My first thought is that maybe I should tell him about the story the old man told me. I have the feeling that he really does want to know what I'm thinking about my "experience" in this place, so I decide, why not? Actually, I would like to get some-body else's opinion about Eichner's story, and this guy seems pretty experienced at dealing with mental patients. I plunge ahead and tell him the whole story about the lottery-picking dog and the stabbing of the neighbor. I tell it just like Eichner told it to me.

Fred listens attentively to the story, and then he sits back in his chair and lets out a low whistle. "Jeez, Scott, that's some story. In fact, a hell of a story. What do you think? Did he really kill his neighbor lady and feed her to his dog? Did you get the feeling he was a dangerous person?"

"No, not really. He said he was telling me the story before it's too late. I'm not sure what he meant by that. Mr. Grimm, the houseparent over there in Cottage H, thought it was because the old man thinks he's going to die."

"Ah, so you got assigned to H. I've heard some weird sto-ries about that ward. Bunch of old guys, some of 'em real old. Some of 'em real strange too. That's what I heard. They call it the permanent ward, and there's a kind of . . . what would you call it . . . mystique about it."

"Well, I don't know about that, but Mr. Grimm did tell me old man Eichner was here a long time ago. But then he left and came back again recently."

Fred looks off into the distance. "Eichner? Sounds German. I don't trust Germans." At that, Fred stops talking and stares down at his now-empty plate. Then he looks up and says, "I think he did it. I bet old man Eichner really did kill his neighbor."

"Do you really? You don't think it was just a made-up story?"

"Nope. It all makes sense. He probably got slapped in this nut house for killing his neighbor."

"But he claims he never got caught. Like I said, he fed the lady's body to his dog."

"Yeah, but what about the bones? He couldn't have got rid of the bones. Humans have some big bones. Think about your hips, for example. And your leg bones. No way he could have got rid of them. He probably buried the bones in his back yard or something. I think you should go back and ask the old man what he did with the bones."

"Really?"

"Sure. Why not? Let's try to figure this out, you and me. It'll be a like solving a murder mystery. A who-done-it. It'll be fun." He glances at his watch. "But I gotta go now. My afternoon class'll be waitin' for me." He gets up. He leans forward with both hands on the table and whispers, "Meet me here at lunch tomorrow and tell me what you find out. Then, we'll make a plan about how to solve this murder mystery."

Seven

Back at the ward, I check in with Mrs. Grimm, but she's busy filling out some kind of official-looking form, and she only nods at me, so I go back to walking around the ward. From now on, I'm determined to just be a good student: observe and learn.

But I do want to ask old man Eichner a few more questions about his story. Maybe I should just ask him straight out to tell me if his story is true. If he says it was, I could ask him for details —like Fat Freddy suggested, like what happened to the woman's large bones?

But I see right away that Eichner is not at his usual bench. I go to the TV-watching area, but he's not there either. I head for Mrs. Grimm to find out where he is.

She's still filling out forms and doesn't look up at me. But I really want to know where the old man went, so I interrupt her: "What happened to Mr. Eichner?"

Still without looking up at me, she says, "Oh, he's out for treatment. He'll be back soon." She continues to fill out the form.

I'm curious about what kind of treatment these patients get, but I can tell she doesn't want me to bother her anymore, so I go back to my boring task of walking and observing.

As I walk through the ward, I immediately sense that something has changed: no one says anything to me, but some of the patients are now watching me, and I could swear their eyes seem angry. And then, as I pass the Growler, who's standing at his usual place against the wall, he not only does his usual growl, he bares the few jagged teeth he has left in his mouth.

I walk on, a bit shaken. What the hell is going on here? Are they all mad at me because I told the Grimms about Eichner's story? But how would they know about that? I wonder if they sent Eichner out for treatment right after I talked to Mr. Grimm? Is his being sent out for treatment just a coincidence? Not likely. And what kind of treatment was he taken out for? When Mr.

Grimm filled me in on ward activity earlier, he never mentioned that patients would sometimes be taken out for "treatment."

I'm about to go back to Mrs. Grimm to try to find out what kind of treatment old man Eichner was taken out for, when I see him being brought back in by two very large men wearing somewhat dirty white uniforms. Eichner looks very pale and shaken. The two men walk him—actually almost drag him—directly back to the dorm.

I hurry to Mrs. Grimm and point toward the dorm. "What happened to Mr. Eichner? He looks terrible."

She looks up from her writing and smiles. "Oh, don't worry about him. He'll be fine."

"But he looks . . . I don't know, like he's hurt or something. He's all pale and shaky."

She waves my concerns off with a dismissive gesture. "Oh that's normal. Don't worry about it."

"Normal for what? He looked really . . . all pale like I said, and . . . hurt."

She cocks her head slightly sideways and stares at me, as if she's wondering why I'm so concerned. "There's always a period of recovery after electroconvulsive therapy," she says. "Nothing to worry about."

"Shock therapy? You shocked him?"

"Now, now, Scott. *We* didn't shock him. Electroconvulsive therapy is up to the doctor. It's part of his treatment regime."

I'm not sure I can go along with her explanation. It's too much of a coincidence that Mr. Eichner got sent out for shock therapy right after I reported what he'd told me. And Mrs. Grimm's dismissive attitude seems too forced. She told me that if I had questions I should bring them to her, but now she's acting like what happened to Eichner is none of my business. And what about the other patients suddenly acting like they're mad at me?

I decide it's a waste of time to ask Mrs. Grimm any more about it, so I go back to walking through the ward. Now none of the patients will even look at me. It's as if they've written me off. Do they now think I'm in league with the Grimms? The Growler has stopped baring his teeth at me, but he still growls every time I pass by. Force of habit, I guess.

Eichner never comes out of the dorm, and with no one to talk to, the time passes slowly. I haven't seen anyone go in there to check on him. Maybe I should go check on him myself. But Mrs. Grimm made it clear that, as a mere student visitor on this ward, it's none of my business.

But what if he's dead back there in his bed? I have to find out.

As I walk past the dorm, I glance in. It's kind of dark in there, so I can't see much, but I still feel like I should go in there and check on him because I can't shake the feeling that it was my fault that he got punished with a shock treatment.

I lean into the dorm and see someone moving about at the very back of the dorm. Is that Eichner back there? I go farther into the room, and as I get closer, I see two men sitting on a bed, talking to another man that's lying face-up in the next bed. I'm pretty sure the man lying in the bed is Eichner, but who are the two men talking to him? They're not elderly, and they're not dressed like patients; they're both wearing dark suits. Who are these two men, and how did they get onto the ward without me seeing them?

One of the men notices me, and they both quickly stand up and walk away. They must have said something to Eichner, because he glances in my direction. Then he turns away and lies perfectly still, as if he's pretending to be asleep.

What was that look Eichner gave me? Accusatory? Or just curiosity, as if he's trying to figure me out. Or figure out which side I'm on?

Hmm. Now why did I have that thought? Are there sides to be taken here on this ward?

Puzzled, I quickly get out of the dorm and go back to walking through the ward, trying to think it all through. Who were those two men in suits? And where did they disappear to? Is there another door back there? No, that can't be; Mr. Grimm said the patients have to ask permission to leave the ward. The front door must be the only way in or out of this ward.

And why did they send Eichner out for shock therapy right after I told the Grimms about the story he told me. Did Mrs. Grimm tell me to go to lunch to get me out of the way?

But would they really use shock therapy as punishment? Just because he told me a story?

But then, maybe Eichner is not just another patient. He doesn't seem crazy, at least not to me. Maybe he's on this ward for some special reason.

Or is it only on this ward that such things are done? Maybe Fat Freddy is right; maybe there really are some strange things going on here in Cottage H.

Eight

The next day, I wake up early and immediately start thinking about Eichner. I wish I could go back to Cottage H to talk to him, but today is the first day of my classes at the U. You'd think the new psychology classes I've signed up for would be all I'd be thinking about, but I can't seem to get the situation at the hospital out of my mind.

I really am looking forward to getting back to school after taking off the whole summer while I waited for the draft lottery results. This will be my first semester as an official psychology major, and I'm a little nervous about how I'll fit in. Do all the other psych majors know each other? Will they see me as an outsider?

I did take that one entry-level psychology course last year. It was intro to behaviorism course that included a lab where I had to train a cute white rat to press a lever. Training that white rat was fun, so after the class was over, I asked if I could take it home with me. As a pet. The teaching assistant who supervised the rat training sessions laughed and said, "We get that a lot. No, the rat will have to be sacrificed."

I couldn't believe what I was hearing. "Sacrificed?" I said. "You mean killed?"

The teaching assistant didn't seem much concerned. He said, "Yeah. We get new rats every semester. They have to be naive for this exercise."

Now you might think my getting to know a cute little white rat that would end up being killed just because I'd successfully trained him to press a lever would have turned me off to the whole field of psychology, but here I am, about to take more psychology courses. I guess if I don't like them, I can always change to some other major next semester.

I park my car and head across campus to the psychology building, diverting around the rowdy anti-Vietnam War protesters that are always gathered at the central fountain, because I know they'd be sure to hassle a draft-age male like me, try to get me to join them.

At the psychology building, I walk the quiet early-morning hallways looking into the empty classrooms. Assuming I don't get drafted and sent to Vietnam, is this where I'm going to spend the next few years of my life?

My only class today is the 400-level clinical practices course I signed up for. That gives me a kind of nervous feeling. Am I up to such an advanced course? The other students will probably be way ahead of me. Maybe I should have signed up for an easier class.

But there's nothing to do about it now except go to the first class and see if I think I can handle it.

It's still early when I find the classroom for the clinical practices course. The empty classroom is a seminar room, with a big old table made of dark wood, surrounded by ten chairs. The professor will probably be sitting at the end of the table that's closest to the door, so I take a seat at the far end.

One by one, the other students start to show up. By the time the class is supposed to start, only seven other students, all males, have come in and taken seats. Looks like it's going to be a small class.

The other students all seem to know each other. They chat together about things like football and what they saw on TV last night. No one speaks to me. I again have the feeling that maybe they won't like an outsider coming into their group. Fine with me; I've never been comfortable meeting new people anyhow.

The professor arrives and takes the seat at head of the table. He's a thin man with thick dark hair and dark eyes. He's wearing a gray suit and a white shirt, but no tie. I wonder if he's a practicing psychologist, but there's no way to know because he just introduces himself as Professor Spence.

He doesn't waste time on formalities; he just opens his notes and begins lecturing about all the treatment methods that have been used, over time, to try to deal with people that had mental problems. He has hurried speech and an impatient manner.

He says, "Archeological evidence indicates that in ancient times someone, perhaps witch doctors, engaged in trepanation. For those of you who don't know, trepanation is the cutting of holes in a person's skull to let out the 'demons' that were assumed to be causing the subject's erratic behavior. Since then, the history of mental-health treatment has been a succession of new hopes followed by disappointing failures. There have been countless new, much-touted, treatments created, but all of them, as we will see in this class, were eventually shown to be worthless. In fact, the search for new treatments of mental problems goes all the way back to the ancient Greeks when scholars of that time described hysteria in women that were showing what they thought of as symptoms. So-called symptoms such as nervousness and fainting. Noting that such problems were only seen in women, Hippocrates of Kos blamed it on a wandering womb. Plato, who was the actual author of the Hippocratic Oath, claimed that if the uterus remains unused beyond its proper time, it gets discontented and angry, and that drives women to extreme behaviors. Consequently, cures for that kind of hysteria were invented, including providing foul-smelling substances to be held under the woman's nose. That was supposed to drive the uterus back to where it belonged."

Nobody is asking questions, maybe because he's talking so fast. And I notice that the other students are all taking rapid notes, and so I realize I'd better start taking notes too.

As he lectures, the professor isn't making much eye contact with any of us students, and if he notices he has a new, unknown student in the class, he doesn't remark on it. But I do notice that he sometimes sneaks a look at me, as if to assess if I'm getting what he's saying. Each time he does that, I make sure I nod thoughtfully, like I'm not only getting it, but also approving of it.

Actually, I am getting it, and that makes me feel a bit more confident that I can handle this advanced course.

Gradually, the professor works his way forward in time to other—but still pretty much misguided—approaches that were attempted in places like Mesopotamia and Egypt. As I listen to him describing the various methods that were used to treat mental illness, I find myself thinking about what I saw yesterday at the mental hospital. I didn't see any actual treatment going on. All I saw at Cottage H was old men silently sitting, acting as if they are totally hypnotized. And the treatment buildings I was shown during my "walk-through" were all completely empty. Actually, the only "treatment" I've seen so far was them sending Eichner out to get shocked.

But the professor hasn't mentioned electroshock therapy. I'm tempted to ask him about that, but nobody else is asking questions, so maybe it wouldn't be appropriate for a new student to be the first one to start asking questions. I would also like to ask him about how those in charge of Cottage H might have been able to get mental patients to sit still all day without making any noise at all. How they could get a whole ward full of mental patients to act like they're totally hypnotized?

Professor Spence continues lecturing about the sordid history of mental treatment until he abruptly stops and says that in the next class he will go through the evolution of more modern mental health treatment systems. He says, "There will be no specific textbook for this course because they are all limited in scope and out of date as soon as they are printed. Instead, I have placed a number of informative books about mental health treatment on reserve at the university library. I expect you to read those books and come to class ready to talk about them."

As I walk away from the class, I'm feeling pretty good about my decision to sign up for a more advanced class. The stuff Professor Spence is lecturing about is quite interesting, and there's no reason I can't keep up with the other students. I walk down the wide hallway, feeling like maybe I really do belong in this building.

I decide to go to the library right now to start reading the books Professor Spence put on reserve there.

At the library, I sign out two of the books he put on reserve. They are both on the history of psychological practice, and one of them is especially interesting because it's about doctors who got famous for coming up with unique mental health treatments that were later discredited. The author of the book is basically suggesting that psychological practitioners should take a cautionary approach to "discovering" new methods of treating mental illness and not get caught up in the idea that there is one "best" method for treating all patients. It makes me think about what I saw in my one day at the mental hospital. The only actual "treatment" I saw was old man Eichner getting sent out for shock therapy. Did one of the doctors there really think that was the best treatment for him? Maybe, but I can't get it out of my head that it might have just been punishment for him telling me a horrific story.

I force myself to concentrate on the book I'm reading, but after a few more hours, I'm feeling sleepy, so I take back the reserve books and check out a few other books on clinical psychology.

At my apartment, I try to study the books, but I find myself nodding off, so I push the book I'm reading aside and lie down. Tomorrow, I'll go back to the mental hospital to continue my "education" there. I wonder how Eichner is doing after his electroshock therapy. As I feel myself getting sleepy, I keep thinking about how shaken Eichner seemed after they brought him back from being shocked. I try to change my mind over to more pleasant thoughts, but it's hard to get that image of how pale and unsteady he was out of my mind. I hope he'll be feeling better by tomorrow.

Nine

It's still dark when I wake up with the remnants of a dream. I think it was some kind of extended nightmare, but I can't remember much of it. In the last part of the dream, I was alone in a darkened room when two big men dressed all in white came in and dragged me out. It felt like I'd broken some kind of hospital rule, and I was being dragged into the shock therapy room "to teach me a lesson."

I open my eyes and stare up into the darkness, trying to remember more of the dream. What did I do that was so wrong that I got shocked? The dream has me feeling worried, but I shake it off. No reason to be worried. At the mental hospital, and the only thing I did "wrong" was report the story Eichner told me. So, why did I dream that it was me getting taken to shock therapy?

The only thing I know about dreams is something I read in a magazine. It was an article about Freud's dream theories. He thought dreams represented unconscious sexual desires that had been repressed. That's a funny idea. More likely that's just the kind of thing he dreamed about. The next time I go to the library, I'll see if I can find some psychology books on dreaming to see what more modern psychologists think about it.

I'm ready to try to get back to sleep when I start remembering those two men I saw talking to Eichner in the dorm. Who were they, and how did they get into the ward? Why did they leave so quickly when they saw me, and why didn't I see them again on the ward later?

Finally, I give up trying to sleep and turn over to look at the clock. It's still dark, but the clock indicates it won't be long before dawn. No one told me I had any set hours for my independent study at the hospital, so I decide I might was well get up and go there.

When I walk onto the ward, the first thing I notice is that the Scribbler is not there at his usual station guarding the front door and taking his imaginary notes.

I cautiously go on into the ward and see something different going on: all of the patients, except for Eichner, are in a line that leads to a small table set up in front of Mr. Grimm's office. On the table are several large bottles, and each bottle contains pills of a different color. Mr. and Mrs. Grimm are both behind the table, and they're handing out pills to each patient in turn. This morning pill-talking session must be a ward ritual that takes place right after the patients get out of bed. The patients shuffle forward to get their daily dose of pills. They all seem to know the routine and are complying like robots. Once again, I'm hit by the same question: how did they train all these men to be so docile? You'd think at least a few of them would resist.

Then I notice something that really surprises me: the Growler is helping. Apparently, his job is to make sure each patient drinks a full paper cup of water to wash the pills down. Then he looks inside each patient's mouth to make sure the pills really have been swallowed. I thought all the Growler did was stand by the wall and growl, but now, with his role in the pill-taking process, he seems to be more "with it" than I thought. Is he some sort of unofficial ward helper?

The Scribbler is also there: he's dragged his chair up next to the Growler and is taking imaginary notes on the whole process. He seems to think it's his duty to document each patient's dose of pills, even though, as always, he's only writing it down with his imaginary pen in his imaginary notebook. I wonder why the Grimms allow it. Maybe they actually encourage his pretending to be the ward note-taker because they think it somehow helps his type of mental illness, whatever it is.

As the pill-giving is being completed, I go back to my usual routine of walking the ward and observing. But this time I'm going to look for clues about what is creating the robotized behavior of these men.

The first thing I notice is that unlike yesterday, when Eichner was taken out for shock therapy and they all stared at me, now none of the patients are paying any attention to me. If I'm supposed to be a fly on the wall, apparently I've succeeded.

After each of the patients has taken his drugs, he goes back to his usual place, either sitting quietly on a bench or at the other end of the room sitting in a chair watching TV.

Wait. Their "usual" places? Why did I have that thought?

I take another trip through the ward, taking note of where each patient is sitting. Yes, I'm sure of it; every single man is sitting in exactly the same place as yesterday. Are they each assigned to a specific seat?

But they were not taken to their seats. How could every one of them not only have an "assigned" place to be, but they also know to go there by themselves? Once again, I'm amazed that all these men have been trained, or forced, to do something like that? Seems impossible. But maybe it's something mental patients do. I should talk to Professor Spence about that.

I assume Eichner must still be in the dorm recovering, so on each of my trips to the far end of the dayroom, I think about going in there to see if he's all right.

But maybe I should just stay out of it and wait to see what happens. Mrs. Grimm made it clear that it's none of my business.

On the other hand, I'm still worried that I was the cause of what they did to him. I look around, and nobody seems to be paying the slightest bit of attention to me, so I duck inside the dorm. I see Eichner, still in the same bed at the far side of the room. He seems to be sleeping. Although I'd sure like to know what happened to him, and who those two man were that I saw with him yesterday, I decide to leave him alone. For now.

I go back out into the dayroom and continue walking. I'm supposed to be observing, but there really isn't much to observe. I find myself wishing Eichner was here to talk to. At least he isn't boring.

It isn't long before Mrs. Grimm starts rounding up the patients.

I'm surprised to see the Growler is helping her get them all into a line. What now?

I soon figure it out: they're lining the men up at the entrance to the dining room. It must be time for their breakfast meal.

Once they get the men all lined up, Mrs. Grimm leads them into the dining room. The Growler brings up the rear, and if anyone straggles, he hurries them along, sometimes roughly pushing them forward. I'm again surprised to see that the Growler has a lot more of a role on this ward than just standing against the wall and growling.

As soon as the Growler has pushed all of the patients into the dining room, I go in too, but I stay by the door. The Scribbler is sitting in a chair just inside the door, and as usual, he's busy taking his imaginary notes. He notices me standing just inside the door, and that triggers even more frantic note taking. He obviously thinks he's doing something important, and his actions so precisely mimic the actions of a real note taker, you'd swear he was actually doing it. Maybe in his mind he's actually writing real words. Is it possible he's memorizing what he pretends to write down?

I see that the men have all seated themselves at the long tables, and each patient has left an empty chair in between himself and the man next to him. That's another thing that indicates some kind of prior training. How did they teach them to do that? Not only that, they're all just sitting there perfectly still, facing toward the front of the room.

Mrs. Grimm moves down the rows placing a plastic bowl in front of each patient. There's some kind of food in those bowls, but nobody has picked up their plastic spoon to start eating. Once again, I'm amazed that they could they have trained them all to act like that. Is it something I don't understand about mental patients?

Finally, Mrs. Grimm, who is now standing at the front of the room, drops her hand, and the men all grab their spoons and start to eat. They seem to be hurrying to eat the food as fast as possible. Are they only given a limited amount of time to eat? And if so, why?

None of this makes any sense. They all look like individuals, but all their individuality seems to have been taken away from them. It feels spookily similar to how I trained my cute little white rat to press a lever. In that class, they taught us how to use positive reinforcement—food pellets—to reward the rat whenever he moved toward the lever. But that was just a rat, and I had full control over the only food he was going to get. This is a large group of mental patients. How could they have been trained to do whatever Mrs. Grimm wants? Are they hypnotized? Or has some kind of punishment been involved?

No sooner do I have that thought when one of the men leans closer to his neighbor, as if to whisper something to him. The Growler is instantly on him, forcefully grabbing the back of the man's neck and pushing his face down into his bowl of food. Then, the Growler forces him to sit up straight while Mrs. Grimm comes to take away his food.

So is that how they keep them all in line? Is the Growler Mrs. Grimm's enforcer?

The Growler was really rough on that old man who is now being forced to sit there without moving even though he has milk and cereal all over his face. It just doesn't seem right to treat an old man like that, even if that's the only way they can keep order on this ward.

I step forward, ready to protest, but Mrs. Grimm gives me a mean look that seems totally out of character from the friendly way she usually acts with me. I'm pretty sure that look is to remind me that I'm only a student observer, and that I should stay out of it. If that's what her look meant, I guess she's right. After all, I am only a student observer, and I really don't know anything about how to deal with mental patients. It's her ward, and maybe this is the only way she can keep these men under control, maybe to keep them from hurting each other. Mr. Grimm said he and his wife had been through some training programs. Maybe they were taught how to use reward and punishment to control the patients, just like I learned to control my experimental white rat. But I never punished my white rat. I was able to get my rat to do what I wanted just by using food as a reward. Maybe using the Growler as the punisher is something the Grimms came up with on their own. If so, it doesn't seem right. I think I'd better keep watching for weird stuff, and later, when I go to lunch, I'll ask Fred about it. And maybe it's another thing I can ask Professor Spence about.

I keep my mouth shut and stay by the door watching the men eat. It's so silent in the room, it feels weird to me, but I can see why. That man was severely punished for trying to talk to his neighbor. Now that I think about it, I don't think I've ever seen any of the patients talk to each other out in the dayroom either. Is talking not allowed on this ward? Is that why Eichner was punished? For talking to me? I keep on having the same thought: how do they manage to enforce such rules? Has the Growler been instructed to watch for any transgression of the rules and deliver the punishment? Is that why, out in the dayroom, he stands there up against the wall, always watching?

The more I learn about the situation on this ward, the stranger it seems. Fred said he'd heard about strange goings on at Cottage H, and now I see that he was right.

I notice one old man who's hands are shaking so much he's having trouble getting the food to his mouth. I hurry to Mrs. Grimm to point that out to her.

She stares at me for a moment, and then she smiles and says, "Why thank you, Scott. Most of them can feed themselves, but a few of them might sometimes need a little help. If you see anybody having trouble, you can help him."

I go to the frail old man and sit down to help feed him. I don't know what he would have done if I hadn't been there to help him get the food into his mouth. The man is so thin, I wonder if he gets enough food to sustain himself. Don't the Grimm's care if one of their patients is slowly starving to death?

The food in the old man's bowl looks like breakfast cereal. And there's nothing else in the bowl besides milk; no fruit or anything else added. Is it some kind of special cereal-like food that has all the nutrients they need?

Somehow I doubt it. It looks like regular old corn flakes to me. I decide to check it out.

But I hesitate: what if they're putting drugs in the stuff?

No, that doesn't seem very likely; they get their drugs in the morning. But I'd sure like to find out what it is. I'm not sure I should be doing it, but Mrs. Grimm isn't watching me, so right after I help the man get the next spoonful of the stuff into his mouth, I snatch a flake out of the bowl and taste it. Yes, I'm pretty sure it's just ordinary corn flakes.

Mealtime doesn't last long. Soon, Mrs. Grimm claps her hands, and all the men quickly get to their feet. One very thin man is still trying to finish eating, but the Growler goes to him and roughly pulls him to his feet.

Then, Mrs. Grimm and the Growler line them all up, and they're marched back into the dayroom. All of them, that is except for the Scribbler. Mrs. Grimm brings him a bowl of cereal, and he's left there to eat by himself. Even though he's quickly eating, he does pause long enough to take a few imaginary notes about me leaving the room.

As I go back to my usual walking the ward, I once again notice that the patients have all gone back to their usual places. As before, none of them are moving, and they're not talking. It's weird, but it's also very boring. I find myself looking forward to going to the employee cafeteria to talk to Fred at noon. I keep checking my watch, and at eleven-thirty, I decide to go. I head for Mrs. Grimm's desk. As usual, she's at her desk filling out some forms, and when I tell her I'm going to lunch, she nods without even looking up.

Maybe she wishes I wasn't here. She seems to have everything so completely routinized on this ward, maybe she'd like to get rid of anything that disrupts that routine, including me.

Ten

Even though I get to the cafeteria building well before noon, Fred is already there waiting next to the door. I wonder if he gets so hungry he comes to the place where the food is early every day, on the off chance that they might open early. He sees me coming and waves happily.

As I arrive, he grins and says, "Well?"

"Well what?"

"Tell me what tall tale the old man came up with this time."

"No tall tale. Actually, I didn't get a chance to talk to him. He was in bed. And here's a weird thing, two men were in the dorm talking to him."

"Two men? Patients?"

"No they were younger men. Wearing suits."

"And you don't know who they were?"

"No. I don't even know how they got onto the ward."

"Hmm. You said Eichner was in bed. Why? Was he sick?"

"No, he was recovering. After I left yesterday, they sent him to electroconvulsive therapy."

"They shocked him? Really? You didn't tell me he was a depressive type."

"He isn't. At least, I don't think so."

"Ha! I bet they shocked the shit out of him because he talked to you about killing his neighbor lady."

"I had that thought too, but it doesn't really make sense. Why would they care if one of the patients told me a crazy story?"

"Hey, maybe he isn't an ordinary patient." Fred stops to think about that for a moment, then he lowers his voice. "The more you tell me about that guy, the more suspicious I get that there's more to him than you think. And I bet it has something to do with that Cottage H. Everybody thinks it's a weird place."

"Why weird? The only thing about it is that they all act really routinized."

"Routinized?"

"Yeah. I wanted to talk to you about that. How did they get those mental patients to do whatever they're told? They're not even allowed to talk to each other."

Fred stares at me as if he can't believe what I'm telling him. He says, "Not ever?"

"No. It's like they've all been trained to not talk or move or anything . It's weird."

Fred frowns. "Doesn't sound like any ward in this nut house I've ever heard about. But like I told you, I've heard that Cottage H is a weird place. But let's get back to our mystery. When you get back to the ward, you should try to talk to old man Eichner about killing his neighbor. See what you can pry out of him."

"I doubt if he'll be getting out of bed today. When they brought him back from shock therapy, he seemed really out of it."

"Oh right. I've seen that before. When they shocked the hell out of one of my teenage students, he didn't come back to school for a week. Not a bad kid. Kind of small for his age."

"Is that right? They shock teenagers too? That's terrible. Did it work? I mean was your student better after that kind of treatment?"

Fred wrinkles up his face. "Depends on what you mean by better. It scared the shit out of him, that's for sure. Made him real quiet and withdrawn. Before they shocked him, he vacillated between being a rowdy kid and being moody and withdrawn. It was like he had two sides to him. Then, after the shocking, there was only one side to him. Always quiet and withdrawn."

"Was? Isn't he your student anymore?"

"Naw. When they turn eighteen, they take them out of the teen ward and send them to an adult ward. And they jerk them out of my class too. I complained that he hadn't caught up with his age group in his studies, but it didn't do any good. They wouldn't let him come back to class. Rules, they said."

"Do you ever see him anymore?"

Fred looks somber and stares down at the ground. "Naw. He killed himself."

"Oh no, Fred. That's too bad. Killed himself on his new ward?"

"No. He escaped and tried to go home. But his father didn't want him. His old man called the cops on him, so the kid ran off and jumped in front of a train. Made a real mess. My students told me they'd heard dogs came from all over to feast on what was left of him. They laughed about that."

Fred gets quiet, and he doesn't seem to want to look at me.

Is he making some kind of sick joke related to Eichner's story about a dog eating human remains? I study his face, but I don't see any indication that he's making up the story. "So that really happened?"

A few more employees are joining the line behind us, but Fred doesn't seem to want to look at them. He lowers his voice: "Yeah. I read about the kid's suicide by train in the newspaper. It was so bad, it even freaked out some of the railroad people. And the newspaper said some of the passengers got sick Had to get psychological help, some of 'em."

I'm trying to think of something to say in response to his horrific story, but they finally open the cafeteria door, and Fred rushes in to go straight for the food.

After Fred's horrible story, I decide against lunch and just get a piece of what looks like apple pie. I go to a table at the back of the room, and when Fred finally joins me with his massive plate of food, I don't even try to talk to him until he's finished polishing it off. Then, he rushes back to the food to fill up his second plateful.

When he comes back, he sits down and lets out a big sigh. "You know, Scotty, it takes a lot of eating for a big guy like me to keep my weight up. Sometimes I think it's not worth it."

I'm pretty sure he's not joking, so I try not to smile at his reference to the hard work of eating. Even if I did laugh at him, I don't think he'd notice. When he eats, he focuses on the food.

I eat my piece of pie slowly, not feeling very hungry because I'm still thinking about Fred's sad story about the boy who'd killed himself.

After Fred has devoured most of the food on his plate, he finally takes a break and looks up at me. "So, the old man is still knocked out from the shock treatment? I bet he's never had it before. When patients have gone through shock treatment a number of times, they bounce back fairly quick. I guess they get used to it."

"That's hard to believe."

"Yeah, well just wait 'til you've been in this place for a while. You see all kinds of things that are hard to believe. Like this one time when one of the younger kids in my class started getting hurt a lot. He'd come in with bruises on his face and scrapes on his arms. I asked him about it, but he just said he thought he was accident prone. It began to happen so often, I asked the other kids about it, and they said he was doing it to himself. Intentionally."

I tried to imagine what Fred is saying. "Why would anybody hurt themselves intentionally?"

Fred shrugs. "Who knows? Maybe he thinks he needs to be punished or something. This is a nut house, right? Maybe hurting himself is why they put him in here."

"Did you talk to him about it?"

"Not allowed. Not long after I got here, I got in trouble for talking to my kids about their mental diagnoses. I thought I might be able to help. But I got called onto the carpet for it. The head nurse reminded me in no uncertain terms that I'm not a shrink, so I shouldn't be trying to act like one. I protested that I was just trying to help. She said, 'Not your job. Better you stick to readin' writin' and 'rithmetic.'"

Fred goes back to eating, and I watch him for a few moments before I say. "Is the kid still doing it? Hurting himself intentionally, I mean."

"Off and on. When he gets down about something, that's when the bruises and scrapes begin, and the other kids start making fun of him. Calling him the head-banger. They laugh about it. I tell them it isn't anything to laugh about, but they don't seem to care what I say. I guess they got their own problems to worry about. Some of 'em have cuts on their arms. Attempted suicides, obviously. One girl has cuts all the way up her arm. The other kids say she's been trying suicide attempts over and over again for a long time. They say it's 'her thing.' I'll tell ya, Scotty, some of my kids come from really horrible home situations. You wouldn't believe the things I hear. And it isn't just the kids. Suicide is a big problem in this whole institution. Haven't you noticed they dress 'em in thick sweatshirts and sweatpants. That way, the patients can't tear up the cloth to make nooses and hang themselves. And no belts or strings allowed. I'm sure you've noticed none of 'em wear shoes. Hospital doesn't want the liability. Lawsuits, you know, if somebody offs themself. Used to be a big problem here in the old days before they got smart about how to prevent it. They got rid of all lamps or other electrical things that have cords. And the TVs are all mounted on the ceilings. Suicides still happen though. If they want to do it, they find a way."

This is turning into a sobering lunch. As Fred continues to eat, I'm thinking about what he's telling me and realize that I actually do now have some things to report back if the university tells me I have to write a report about what I've learned in my mental hospital "experience." But do I want to repeat such horrible stories?

Fred finishes eating and says he has to get back to his afternoon classes. But before he goes, he again encourages me to talk more to Eichner. "We've got to get to the bottom of this mystery," he says. "You and me working together. We'll figure it out."

Eleven

Walking back to Cottage H, I think about doing what Fred said. Maybe I *can* get more out of Eichner, assuming he's not still in bed, recovering. Maybe I should tell him I like his stories and try to get him to tell me more.

As soon as I walk onto the ward, and get past the Scribbler, I see Eichner is back, sitting on his usual bench, and he's looking at me. After I check in with Mrs. Grimm, I go straight to Eichner and sit on his bench next to him. "Well," I say, "you seem to be feeling better."

He stares at me for a long moment before he responds. "Oh, did you think I was sick?"

"Well, you weren't looking so good that last time I saw you."

He turns away from me. "No thanks to you. I told you not to tell anybody."

So he does blame me for him getting punished, assuming that's what the shock treatment was all about. "But Mr. Eichner, I'm only a student observer here. Aren't I supposed to tell Mrs. Grimm about what I see and hear on this ward?"

He turns back and looks right into my eyes. "Not if you want to know my secrets. They are strictly between you and me."

Under the glare of his pale blue eyes, I feel like a chastened schoolboy. I lean closer to him and whisper, "All right, Mr. Eichner, we'll just keep our little talks between the two of us."

He continues to stare at me. Then he frowns and looks away. "I don't know if I can trust you."

"Trust me? Trust me about what?"

"About what I was planning to tell you. Something important, something that has to be done right away, before it is too late."

So, he's doing the "too late" thing again. I'm beginning to wonder if it really is about him being afraid of dying. But that's what Mr. Grimm thought, and what else could it be? I decide to just come right out and ask him. "Too late? What does that mean, Mr. Eichner?"

He looks at his fingernails, as if examining them for dirt. But they're clean. In fact, they're remarkably clean.

He leans closer and whispers, "I need something important done. And it must be done before time runs out." He touches my shoulder with one finger, very gently. "Are you willing to help me? You might find it very rewarding."

Very rewarding? That seems like a weird thing for him to say. Maybe I shouldn't get any more involved in this, but I am curious, so I say, "Remember, Mr. Eichner, I'm only a visiting student here. I don't have any authority on this ward, so I don't think I can do anything for you."

"It is not about this ward, son. It is about my house."

"Your house?"

"Yes, I need something from my house."

Does he expect me to go to his house to get something for him? Is that allowed? Maybe I should ask Mrs. Grimm about that. No, that might get Eichner sent to shock therapy again. I'd better hear what he has to say and then ask Fred about it when I see him. But then, if I tell Fred, he'll get really interested and want to get involved. He'll want to go to straight to Eichner's house "to investigate."

Eichner is still looking at me, waiting for my response.

"Are you saying you want me to go to your house and get something for you?"

"That is correct."

"Well, I guess it, uh, depends on what it is."

"Oh, it is nothing of importance. That is, not to anybody but myself. A small thing. Not of great consequence."

Not of great consequence? I don't believe that. His attempts to allay my concerns has got me even more concerned. "Well, I don't know, Mr. Eichner. If you need somebody to bring you something from your home . . . I mean, don't you have any relatives that could fetch if for you?"

He shakes his head. "No relatives. All dead. Long gone. You are my only hope."

I know I shouldn't even be thinking about doing such a thing for a patient, especially since I don't really know the rules here. I turn to look toward Mrs. Grimm, but thankfully, she's totally involved in her paperwork and doesn't seem to notice me talking to Eichner.

I turn back to him. "How about you just tell me what it is you want, and I'll see what I can do."

"Well, son, it is not that simple. It is at my house, but it is hidden in a safe place there."

"It's hidden?"

"Yes, you will have to locate it and then bring it to me. Just think about it as a little errand. And as I said, you will be richly rewarded."

Now he's saying I'll be *richly* rewarded. Well, if he's talking about money, I sure could use it. But does he really have money? Why would a patient in this kind of publicly-funded institution have money? In fact, Mr. Grimm told me this was a place for old men who had no relatives and no money. And maybe more important, why would Eichner be offering a "rich" reward if the task is so simple?

"I can see you are suspicious," he says. "But you have no need to be. As I said, the matter is not of great importance, but the time is urgent. I just need someone to go to my house and get something I hid there. Before it is too late."

"Too late for what, Mr. Eichner?"

He winks at me. "That is an aspect of the secret, son. You will see when you get there." He reaches into his pocket and pulls out a piece of paper. On the paper is what looks like a street address and a pencil drawing of a square with an "X" inside of it. I ask, "Is this the address of your house. Is it in this city?"

"Yes it is. Do you think you can find it?"

"Sure. But what is this square with an X drawn inside of it?"

"That is the location of what I want you to get for me. Inside of my house." He reaches out and taps on the piece of paper. "I repeat, it is not, as you young people would say, a big deal. It is a minor thing that I had to leave behind at my house when I came here, but now I would like to have it back." He taps the paper again. "The square represents the attic of my house, and the X is the location of the thing I need you to bring to me."

"Now wait a minute, Mr. Eichner. If this thing is so important, why didn't you bring it with you when you came here? And how do you know it's still there?"

Eichner leans closer again and whispers, "I could not bring it to a place like this, so I hid it in my attic. I know it must still be there because I hid it well. It is under the floor where that X shows. You will have to move a large cabinet to get to it, but you are young and strong. It should be no trouble for you."

"Well, I don't know, Mr. Eichner. Maybe you should ask somebody else to go get it for you."

He shakes his head. "I have no one. And even if I did, I trust no one. It is as I said, a secret, just between the two of us."

He's saying the thing is of no great consequence, but it has to be a secret. "A secret?" I ask. "What kind of secret, Mr. Eichner?"

He winks again. "Now if I told you, it would no longer be a secret, would it?"

Is this old man playing some kind of trick again with all this talk about a secret and some kind of urgency? I'm beginning to think I shouldn't get any further involved with this old man, no matter what Fred thinks.

Eichner quickly stands up and walks away from me.

Where is he going? I look around and see that Mr. Grimm is standing outside the door to his apartment. I'm pretty sure he's been watching me, and he doesn't look too happy about me talking to Eichner again. I sure hope I haven't earned Eichner another shock treatment.

I look back and see that Eichner is hurrying into the dorm. Can he go in there anytime he wants to? I haven't seen any other patient do that.

I get up and go back to walking the ward, trying to look innocent.

As I pass by Mr. Grimm, he frowns, but he doesn't say anything to me. He whispers something to his wife, and then he goes back into his apartment.

Mrs. Grimm continues doing her paperwork, but now, she's keeping her eye on me.

As I walk, none of the other patients are paying any attention to me, except for the Scribbler, of course, who's taking copious imaginary notes about my trips back and forth past him. The Growler continues to growl at me every time I pass by him, but I've gotten so used to that, I hardly notice it anymore.

It's not long before Eichner comes back to sit on his usual bench

He doesn't even glance at me as I pass by him. Fine with me. I'm no longer sure I want to have anything to do with him. After all, I'm only supposed to be here to observe and learn. I'll be better off just sticking with that and not doing anything that might compromise my independent study credit. On my next trip past Eichner, I should just hand him back his piece of paper and tell him I'd rather not get involved.

But as I approach him on my next trip through the ward, he winks at me and smiles.

Now, what is that wink supposed to mean? Does he think we're coconspirators now?

I decide to not let my face give away anything. I just walk right past him without even a glance. I'm not sure what he's up to, but I won't let him talk me into doing anything that could get me into trouble.

But I will hang onto the piece of paper he gave me. The least I can do is go check it out.

But what am I thinking? Why would I do that? I'm not sure what Eichner is up to, but whatever it is, I'm better off staying completely clear of it. And I'd better not even tell Fred about it either. If I tell him Eichner gave me the address of his house and said there was some mysterious, maybe-valuable, thing there, Fred would for sure want to go with me to "solve the mystery." On the other hand, after I finish here, I should at least go see what Eichner's house looks like. I can check to see if the neighbor lady's house and yard look anything like he described it in his story. That'll tell me if that part of his horrific murder story might be true. Then I can talk to Fred about what I saw, if I decide to.

Twelve

After I leave the hospital, I decide now might be the best time to take a quick drive by Eichner's house. I don't have anything else to do, and besides, there's no harm in just seeing what his house looks like. But no matter what he said about something valuable being hidden in his house, I know I'd better not get involved in it. Eichner might have just been playing a joke on me. And besides, even if there really is something hidden in his house, it's not up to me to get it. Better to just stay out of the whole thing.

Using my driving map of the city, it doesn't take me long to find the street Eichner wrote on the piece of paper. But when I get there, I'm in for a surprise: the street ends at a tall chain-link fence with nothing behind it but dirt and rubble. A lot of heavy equipment is sitting around over there. It looks like they've torn out the entire neighborhood. Are they getting ready to put in a big new development? No wonder Eichner said "before it's too late." Well, it's already too late, Mr. Eichner. It looks like you're house is gone; in fact, your whole damn neighborhood is gone.

As I look at the plowed-up dirt field and the huge piles of mangled lumber and other destroyed building materials behind that tall fence, I realize Fred is going to be really disappointed. He wanted to play detective and go look for the dead woman's bones at Eichner's house, but now there's no way to do that: the houses have already been bulldozed.

I wonder why they decided to tear down this particular neighborhood. There's nobody around to ask, but there is a coffee shop across the street. I decide to go there and ask if anybody there knows what's going on.

I take off my professional-looking jacket and put on my black hoodie, and then I go to look in through the coffee shop's big front window. There's only one person inside, a young woman who's sitting at one of the tables reading a book. Is she a patron or an employee? She's not dressed in a uniform like a waitress; she's just wearing jeans and an athletic-type blue sweatshirt. She's about my age, dark-haired, and kind of nice looking.

As I go into the coffee shop, the girl stands up. She looks me over, and the way she's staring at me with her light blue eyes feels kind of unnerving. She seems to be sizing me up. Does she do that to everybody that comes into this place, or is it something about me?

"Oh, sorry," she says finally. "I wasn't expecting anybody this time of day. Do you want some . . . uh, some coffee or something. I could make it in a jiffy."

I shake my head. "No, I was just looking at—"

"It'll only take me a minute. It's only that all the demolition workers have gone home, so I didn't think I was going to get anymore business today. If you want some coffee, all I have to do is put the grounds in the thing and then some water in the other thing and turn it on. It makes coffee okay. Nothing fancy, just regular coffee. This is not one of those fancy coffee places. It's just . . . you know, regular coffee."

"No thanks. I was just looking at the heavy equipment and the demolition going on across the street. What's that all about?"

"Oh, that's War Town. Was War Town, I should say. At least that's what everybody around here called it. They're tearing it all down, lock stock and barrel. No need for it anymore. Gonna build a great big shopping center over there. All kinds of different stores, they say. Big ones and little ones. All kinds of stores. By the way, my name's Jill. I know Jill is a silly name. Like going up the hill for a pail of water and all that. But it's actually short for Jillianna which isn't much better, but what can I say? Blame my mother. She named me that. Said it was a name she heard in Europe somewhere. That's where they are now, she and my dad. Europe. Actually, Belgium. Last I heard. Peace Corps, you know. Or didn't you know they have grownups too? Yeah, two years at a stretch. So I stay with my granddad while they're off gallivanting around the world. He's the one who actually owns this coffee shop. I keep telling him he's wasting his money keeping the place open just for a few demolition workers, but he thinks once the shopping center opens, he'll get a lot more customers. I told him they'll have their own coffee shops over there, but of course he never believes anything I say." She stops talking and blinks a few times, and then she shrugs. "I talk too much don't I? Are you sure you don't want some coffee? Or something to eat? Actually, all I have left is coffee. We had some donuts, but the workers ate 'em all."

She finally stops talking long enough to take a breath, which gives me time to respond to her. "Uh, no thank you, Jill. For the coffee, that is. Actually, I think Jill is a nice name, Mine's Scott, by the way. I'm a student. You know, up at the university."

"Oh," she says, "I want to go to college too. If I can ever get enough money to do it. What are you majoring in?"

"Psychology. Uh, now."

"Oh, a psych major. That's a good thing. I suppose you're analyzing me right now."

"Oh, no," I say quickly. "Actually, I'm just getting started as a psych major. But I am doing uh . . . a special kind of psychology study at the local mental hospital. Anyhow, that doesn't matter. What I came in to find out about was what they're doing over there across the street. All that demolition going on over there. Did you say it was called War Town?"

"Yes, it was. Uh, why don't you have a seat, and I'll tell you about it."

I sit down at the table, and she sits across from me.

"It was called War Town, like I said. At least that's what us kids used to call it. There used to be a munitions plant nearby. During the war. The second world war, that is, not the one going on now over there in Vietnam. Back then, they built at lot of houses over there for the workers. That's when Granddad opened this coffee shop. Did okay back then. I wasn't even born yet, of course, but when I did get born, I used to play with some of the kids over there. I only live a few blocks from here. But you probably don't care about that. Anyhow, after the war was over, the munitions plant closed down and the workers moved away, and

the neighborhood got all run down. At least that's what my granddad says. Then, refugees from the war moved in. Poles, Jews,
Hungarians. Whole bunch of them. Even some Germans. All living over there like it was the United Nations. Except my granddad says they weren't all that united. You know, trouble between
the Germans and the Jews. Actually, between the Germans and
everybody else. World war two, you know. But with the munitions plant closed down, most everybody left to find jobs somewhere else, and the place got even more run down. Like I said,
the neighborhood only existed in the first place because of that
war. Oh, there I'm doing it again. Started talking too much. I
know, I know, I talk too much. My grandad tells me that all the
time. Now, what was it you said you wanted? Coffee? Did you
say your name is Scott? That's a good name. A good solid name.
Don't you want some coffee, Scott?"

"Uh, no thanks to the coffee. And I don't think you talk too
much. You told me what I wanted to find out. About why they're
tearing everything out behind that fence over there, I mean."

"Why?"

"Why what?"

"Why did you want to know about it? Why did you want to
know about War Town?"

"Oh, right. Well, I met this old guy at the mental hospital
where I've been working. He wrote down his address for me." I
take out the piece of paper Eichner gave me and show it to her.
"He doesn't know his house is already torn down."

She takes the piece of paper and looks at it carefully.
"Actually, it may not be. Not torn down yet I mean."

"Really? Why not?"

She points to the address on the paper. "This address. Does
your old man friend happen to be German?"

"Uh, yes. I think maybe he is. At least his name sounds
German. Eichner."

"Well then, he must be the one fighting it. What I mean is, I
heard—that is, the workers told me—that some old German guy
is fighting them tearing down his house. Fighting it in court."

"In court? He . . . uh, doesn't seem like the type to do that. But then, I don't actually know him very well."

"Well, if it is his house, it's one of the biggest houses in War Town. Two stories tall. An old fashioned kind of place. Tall front porch columns and everything. I know that house well. We used to play in a vacant lot near it. When we were kids, I mean. Everybody talked about that house back then. Supposed to be some mean old German living there. Anyhow, that's what the older kids said. We ran away whenever he came out onto his front porch. Like I said, the workers told me some old German guy is fighting tearing down his house because it's historic. Says it should be on the national historic register of old houses. But he'll lose. That's what the workers told me. Can't fight big business, they said. So I guess they'll tear down that house any day now."

So Eichner knew what he was talking about when he said his little task needed to be done before it's too late. He meant before his house is torn down. But how could Eichner, a patient in a mental hospital, be fighting it in court?

I turn to look out the coffee shop's big front window. The sun is getting low in the western sky, but I think I do see what looks like a large white house in the distance." I point. "Is that it? That big white house in the distance?"

"Yeah. That's it. The others are all torn down. Actually, I shouldn't tell you this, but I was inside the fence the other day. Just looking around. But I didn't go into that house."

"You got through the fence?"

"Sure. No problem. Didn't I say I grew up only a few blocks from here? There's a ravine where we used to play hide and seek. Brambles and bushes and lots of places to hide down in that ravine. I'm skinny enough to crawl in under the fence from down there. I think you could get in too, if you want to. You're tall, but thin enough I think. Wanna see it?"

I hesitate. Now that I know Eichner's house is about to be torn down, I'm starting to feel a lot more curious about checking it out before it's too late. Maybe I should just go in there, do a quick search, and get right back out. But do I really want to do that? What if I got caught? "Uh, won't they have some kind of guard in there?"

"They did, an old man. But now that just about everything has been torn down, they got rid of him. Nobody in there at all, last time I went in."

She seems confident that she has a way to get on the other side of the fence. Maybe she's something of a risk taker. But then, do I really want to get involved in one of Eichner's stories? Who knows what he's actually up to.

Jill is staring at me. "Well, don't you want to go in and see?"

"It's . . . uh, complicated. I'm not sure I can believe anything the old man, Eichner, told me."

"So what? Let's just go in and look around. I don't have anything else to do. Do you?"

"Well, not really."

"So, why not? It'll be an adventure. Like when we were kids. We'll sneak in and see what the mystery is about that old house."

Jill seems excited, She's ready to do it right now. But should I let her talk me into something like this? On the other hand, I wouldn't mind getting to know her better, and going for an adventure with her might be a great way to do it. "Uh, what time do you close?"

She stands up. "I can close right now. Nobody's going to come in anyhow. Let's go. I'll show you where the ravine is."

Jill closes up the cafe, and then she leads the way to an overgrown ravine. It doesn't look like there's a path through the heavy brush, but she leads me on down a twisting and turning route through the bushes that eventually takes us to the bottom of the ravine. There, the thick brush seems even more impenetrable, but every time we get stuck, she manages to find a narrow way through. She must have done this a thousand times.

From there, she leads me up through the ravine until, eventually, we come to the fence. She shows me how to lie down on my back and squirm under it, and we're in.

As soon as we're through the fence, I see devastation everywhere—big stacks of broken-up lumber, wiring, shingles, and pipes pushed together, apparently by bulldozers. They must be going to haul the stuff off somewhere else to go through it to find anything of value.

In the long late-afternoon shadows, the whole place feels kind of quiet and spooky, and I'm starting to have second thoughts about being in here. "Are you sure we won't get arrested for trespassing?"

"Naw. Like I told you, there's nobody in here at night."

I hope she's right. I say, "Okay. Where's the house?"

"Over there." She points.

I see it in the distance. It really is the only house still standing, and it looks extra large, standing alone amidst all the devastation.

When we get closer, I see that it's an old two-story frame house, taller than it is wide. It actually looks kind of grand, mostly because of its oddly out-of-place tall white columns on the front porch. But the place is starting to get pretty run down. Apparently, it used to be white, but its flaking paint is getting dingy-looking. And there are brown rust streaks running down the sides from rusted-out holes in the sagging gutters along the roof.

The silent and austere old house feels oddly . . . threatening. I wonder why I'm having those kinds of feelings about it? Is it because I'm remembering the horrific story Eichner told me about killing his neighbor lady? Or, maybe it's just that all abandoned old houses feel spooky.

Jill must not be having those kinds of feelings, because she leads the way right up onto the porch. But then she suddenly stops and puts out her hand to hold me back. "Uh oh," she says. "Looks like somebody's beat us to it." She points to the sagging front door that seems to have been partly kicked loose. It's barely hanging in place by only one hinge.

I say, "Maybe the demolition workers."

She shakes her head. "I doubt it. All of the houses were cleaned out a long time ago. This is the last one, and it's ready to be torn down.

"Okay," I say. "We don't have to go in. I was just curious."

She turns to look at me. "You don't want to go in? Now that I showed you how to get in under the fence?"

The way she said it makes me think she's decided I'm chicken. Is this like one of her childhood adventures where she gets to be the leader? "Well," I say, "let's just go in for a quick look around."

She laughs and shrugs. "No, we don't have to. For a minute there it was like I was a kid again, and this was our latest adventure. Like I said, all the other kids were scared of this house. You know what kids are like. Scare stories about the old German. And if he heard us outside, he'd come out onto his front porch and yell at us. We'd go running away."

Her words make me wonder if the kids had heard something about a murder. Kids sometimes know things the adult world doesn't know anything about. I say, "No, I'm willing if you are. Let's go in."

"Right. Let's go."

She squeezes in through broken door, and I cautiously follow.

The house is completely empty. There's not a bit of furniture in the place and no pictures on the walls. But I can tell it used to be a fairly nice house. Sad to think of it being turned into rubble and hauled away to some landfill.

The fancy-looking wallpaper in the front hallway is shredded, as if somebody's been tearing at it. But why would anybody do that?

Jill is already heading into the next room, so I follow. She's very silent as we walk through the rooms. Is she having memories of what these old houses were like when she was a kid, back when it was called War Town?

She leads us into what must have been the living room. Almost all of the windows in this room are cracked, and a few of them are completely broken out. Probably kids throwing rocks before the demolition company put up the fence to keep everybody out.

As we walk through the downstairs rooms, there's not a sound except for the crunching of glass under our feet. There's a bit of fine dust floating in the air that's especially noticeable with the rays of late-afternoon sunlight that are slanting in through the broken windows. It gives the whole place a sort of orangish glow.

As we explore, Jill is being silent for a change. I wonder if she's having the same kinds of spooky feelings I am about this place, and I don't think it's only me remembering Eichner's story about him committing a murder here; there's also a weird feeling that I think is related to the house itself. Maybe it's only because it feels so empty and . . . abandoned. Maybe abandoned old houses always feel this way, but somehow I doubt it. The house seems to be giving off a noticeable feeling of . . . sadness. For the first time, now that I've seen his house, I'm going to have to agree with Fred—Eichner probably really did kill his neighbor lady. And I think he really did keep her body in this house for a long time.

Jill leads us into another smaller room. Here too, the old wallpaper is faded and shredded. This room is not quite empty: there's a chandelier made of dangling glass beads that reflect the sunlight coming in through the window. It was probably a pretty nice thing in its day, maybe even valuable, but it seems to have lost a lot of its glass beads. It's been partly pulled down out of the ceiling. I wonder if somebody tried to pull it down to steal it. It's hanging slightly askew which gives the whole room a feeling of being slightly off kilter. Maybe it used to be some kind of sitting room. I imagine Eichner spending a lot of time all alone in this room, with only his loyal dog Adolph for company.

Next, we go into the kitchen. The large sink is scratched and very dirty. Is this where Eichner cut up the neighbor lady? If he really did kill her, it would have taken him a long time to cut her up and feed her to his dog, a little bit more every day. And as he did it, he was probably always waiting for that knock on the door when the police would come. Was he always afraid of that?

But as soon as I have that thought, I doubt it. I can't even imagine Eichner being afraid of anything. He may be an old man, but every time I've talked to him, he always seems as cool as the proverbial cucumber. Jill said this place was called "War Town," and she said at one time it was inhabited by refugees from World War Two. Maybe Eichner was in that war. Maybe he saw some horrific things over there, so now nothing is likely to rattle him.

Jill is staring at me. "You're being very quiet. What're you thinking about?"

"Oh, I was thinking about the old man who used to live here."

"Oh right, you said you know the old man who lived in this house."

"Actually, I just met him the other day."

That makes her stop and stare at me. "You hardly know him, but you wanted to get into his house?"

"Yeah, well, it's kind of . . . complicated."

She's still staring at me. Does she think I'm a weird person? I don't want her to think that, so I quickly say, "Even though I just recently met him, we talked quite a bit. And he told me some . . . well, let's just say some interesting stories about this old house.

She nods thoughtfully, and then shrugs. "Okay, well then, let's keep looking. She leads me into the next room. She stops and points at the wall. "Look. Holes."

I turn to see what she's pointing at. Whole sections of wallboard have been chopped out between the framing, probably with an ax or something.

"Those holes are new," says Jill.

"Really? You think so?"

"Yeah. Look close. Don't they seem new to you?"

She's right. The chopped edges of the holes are not dusty like everything else. Somebody else has been in this house, probably whoever kicked the front door loose. I whisper, "Maybe they're still here."

Jill shakes her head. "It's deadly quiet in this old house. We would have heard them."

I point to the holes and say, "They were obviously looking for something."

She frowns. "In the walls? Like what?"

I have the strong feeling that it was somebody looking for the same thing I'm looking for. But I don't say that. Instead, I say, "The demolition workers maybe?"

Jill says, "No, they wouldn't chop holes in the walls. They're just going to knock the whole house down anyhow. They haul it all away, and then they pick through it all to find the stuff they can sell." She turns to stare at me. "Well?"

"Well what?"

"Are you going to tell me what's really going on here? The place is empty. It's going to be torn down. But somebody is chopping holes in the walls, like they want to find something before that happens. You never said exactly why you wanted to look inside this old house. What are we actually looking for?"

I figure I might was well tell her the truth. If I don't, she'll think I don't trust her, and she'll probably regret that she brought me in here in the first place. "Actually, I'm here looking for something that old man Eichner wanted me to come here to get for him. Before they tear his house down."

"Get something? What?"

"That's the odd thing. I don't know. He wouldn't tell me. Here, look again at the paper he gave me." I take Eichner's piece of paper out of my pocket and show it to her. "See that X inside the square he drew? The square is this house, and the X stands for what he wanted me to get."

"Well, where is it?"

"He said it was hidden up in the attic."

"In the attic?"

"That's what he said. He gave me the idea that it might be valuable.

"Well, let's go find it."

"Uh . . . okay."

She immediately leads the way. No hesitation at all, despite seeing those chopped-out holes in the wall.

I follow, amazed at how unafraid she is. She's a brave one all right. Sneaking in through that ravine and under the fence. And then she headed straight through all the rubble like it was a walk in the park.

She leads the way to the stairs that lead up to the second floor, but then she stops. "The steps are gone."

She's right. Every single one of the steps has been removed. "The steps aren't broken," I say. "They've been pried up, one by one. It's another indication that somebody was looking for something."

"But you said it was hidden in the attic, whatever it was."

"Yeah, but they must not have known that, so they were looking in every place Eichner could have hidden something."

Jill grins. "All the more reason we should try to get up into the attic. We can still get up these stairs if we hang onto the banister and be careful to only step on the wood braces."

She begins working her way up, and I follow. The torn-up steps might very well mean whatever Eichner hid in this house really *is* something valuable.

Halfway up, Jill holds up her hand to stop me. She says, "Listen."

I stop moving, and I do hear something. A scurrying sound. "I say, "It's coming from the second floor, or maybe up in the ceiling."

Jill says it before I can: "Rats, probably. Or some other kind of critters up there."

But she keeps working her way up and I follow.

The rooms on the second floor turn out to be as empty as the ones downstairs. And some of the walls have been chopped into, just like downstairs.

Jill points that out, but doesn't say anything.

As we walk through the empty rooms looking for access to the attic, I notice the hardwood floors, that were apparently once highly polished, are now dull, and the cracks between the boards

are clogged with old dirt. How long has this place been abandoned? Eichner hasn't been at the mental hospital all that long, so
if he hasn't been here in this house, where has he been? Maybe
the cops weren't done with him after all. Maybe he was on the
run before he showed up at the mental hospital. That gives me a
startling thought: maybe Eichner is *hiding out* at Cottage H. Mr.
Grimm did say Cottage H was a place where old men ended up
when they had no place else to go to and nobody to take care of
them. He made it pretty clear that he expected the old men in
Cottage H to remain there for the rest of their lives. For an old
man on the run, Cottage H could be the perfect place to hide out.
That thought gives me a whole new way to look at Eichner. No
wonder he doesn't act like the other patients. But surely the
Grimms, being experienced mental hospital houseparents, would
notice that too. Something about it just doesn't make sense.

As I walk down the long hallway, the wood floors make eerie
creaking sounds with each of my steps. I realize Jill has fallen
behind. I turn and say, "You don't have to come with me if you
don't want to."

She waves for me to go on, still silent, which I'm sure is
unusual for her.

After I've opened every door on the second floor, I'm beginning to wonder if there really is an attic. The house is tall enough
to have an attic, but there is no door with stairs leading upward. I
check every closet to be sure there's no secret door. Nothing.
Could Eichner have been making the whole thing up?

"There's no door to the attic," I say. "If there really is an attic

She points up at the ceiling. "What about that?"

I see what she's looking at. There's a kind of handle, recessed
into the ceiling. I say, "Yeah, it could be a trapdoor. Let's take a
look."

Jill stares up at it. "Okay, how?"

She has a point. There's nothing to stand on to reach up to
that high ceiling. I say, "We need a stepladder or something."

"I don't think we'll find anything like that around here.
Besides, it's going to get dark out there pretty soon."

"Yeah. I guess I could get a stepladder and come back tomorrow."

"You can't come in when the workers are here. And I bet they're gonna knock this place down tomorrow morning."

I look back at Jill and say, "Well, I guess there's only one possible solution, isn't there?"

She looks up at the ceiling and then back at me. "You promise you won't drop me?"

"I promise."

She smiles and says, "Well, okay. Let's do it."

She slips off her shoes, and I link my fingers together. She steps into my hands, and I lift her up. It's surprisingly easy; she seems to weigh hardly anything.

I say, "Can you get it?"

"I've got ahold of the handle, but it seems to be stuck."

She's taking so long, my hands are starting to ache. We may have to give up on this approach. After all, I did promise not to drop her.

Finally, she says, "Got it."

She pulls down, and it starts to come loose. It really does seem to be a trapdoor. She gives it one more jerk, and it comes completely loose. I get a face full of old dust, and I expect she did too. I barely manage to hang onto her as she pulls down what turns out to be a hanging set of metal stairs. Unlike everything else in this old house, the metal stairs seem to be as new and shiny as the day they were made.

I lower Jill down, and we both stand there looking at the hanging metal stairs.

"Well," she says, "this is interesting. We don't really know what's up there, but I think we should go up and see."

She starts to get onto the hanging steel steps, but I grab her arm to hold her back. "No, it's my deal. I'll go first."

The stairs sway a bit as I go up, but they seem to be attached firmly.

I make it up, and sure enough, it is a large attic, tall enough to stand up in. It's dark, but there is one small window at the far end, and some sunlight is coming in through it.

I reach down to help Jill.

Once she's up, she says, "It's dusty up here. Nothing up here but dust and mouse poop."

"Dusty is right, but look here." I point to a set of footprints in the dust. They lead to the far wall, and sure enough, a whole section of that wall has been chopped away, just like downstairs."

"So, somebody else has been up here," she says. "And still looking for something hidden in the walls. But what is that terrible smell? Something dead. I don't like it. We should get out of here."

"It sure does smell like rotting flesh," I say. I have the sudden memory of Eichner describing how he cut up his neighbor lady. Could he have hidden pieces of her in the walls? Is that why somebody has been chopping holes in the walls? No, that's crazy. Eichner said he put her into his freezer. Something else is dead up here.

My foot touches something, and I jump back.

"What is it?" Jill says grabbing my arm. For the first time, she sounds scared.

I lean down for a closer look. "It's a rat. A dead rat. Probably lots of dead ones up here. That's what smells so bad."

"I hate rats," says Jill. "One time, when I was real little, we got a bunch of rats in our house. They were living in the ceiling. We couldn't figure out how they were getting in. Turns out, it was a wire. They were crawling across a wire from the telephone pole and getting into the attic. My dad had to put up a piece of screen to stop them, but that only trapped them up there. We smelled them for months."

"Rats need food and water," I say. "From the looks of this one, it seems his buddies have been eating him."

Jill turns up her nose. "Ick. Let's get out of here."

"Right. Just let me look around for a minute. He said there'd be a large cabinet."

Jill points. "The only furniture up here is that thing. Looks like a big bar or something. I think it's attached to the wall."

I go closer. It is pretty big, but Eichner said it could be moved. "Let me try to move it," I say. I give it a hard push, and it doesn't move at all. Maybe she's right, and it is built in. But why would Eichner tell me I could move it? I say, "Come on, Jill, let's try it together."

We both get our hands on it, and we push, but there's no sign the thing is going to budge. I say, "Maybe it's just stuck. Let's try one more time. Really hard this time. Ready? On three. One, two, three, push."

I push as hard as I can, and Jill must be pushing hard too because amazingly, the thing does move a few inches. I say." Ha! It's not attached. We can move it."

She's frowning. "Maybe. But that was as hard as I can push."

"Listen, Jill, now that we're up here, don't you want to know what's under this thing?"

She just stares at me, her hands on her hips. "Are you sure you don't know what we're looking for?"

"I wish I did. I'm ready to get out of this house as much as you are, but if they really are going to tear this house down tomorrow, and we've come this far, we might as well try to find it. Whatever it is. You never know, it might be something really interesting. Maybe even really valuable."

She hesitates for a moment, and then she grins and rubs her hands together. "Let's do it."

I say, "Ready, set, go, push!"

We both push hard, and this time, with a squeaking of wood sliding on wood, the big old thing actually moves relatively easily. It must have just been stuck. We've managed to move it enough to reveal a square pattern cut into the wood of the floor that was under it. We both get down on our knees to look at it. The square pattern must have been cut into the floor with a very thin cutting blade. I say, "It must be a hidden compartment under the floor." I pick at it with my fingernails, but if it is a compartment, it doesn't seem to want to come loose. We need some kind of tool, but there's nothing at all in the attic that could be used to pry it up, and I don't remember seeing anything downstairs that would work as a prying tool.

But Jill doesn't seem ready to give up. She begins clawing at it with her fingernails, and sure enough, she gets it to lift a little. I join in, and pretty soon, we get a rectangle of wood to pop loose. I set it aside and look down into the darkness. "Nothing but floor joists."

Jill frowns. "After all this, and there's nothing here. Is it some kind of joke?"

I hope old man Eichner isn't pulling another one of his tricks out of his sleeve.

Jill is looking down into the darkness. "Maybe somebody beat us too it. Remember those holes chopped in the walls."

I shake my head. "No, there are footprints in the dust up here, but it's obvious this big counter hasn't been moved until we moved it." I lean forward to look down into the hole. "It's kind of dark down there. Should we reach down and feel around?"

Jill holds up both hands. "Not me. I'm afraid of spiders. Once, I reached into a cardboard box in Granddad's garage and felt something crawl on my hand. I jerked my hand right back out and went to get a flashlight. Guess what it was. A black widow spider. I don't know why it didn't bite me."

She has a point, but I'm not going to leave until I find out if there's something down in the hole between the floor joists. It could be something very small that we can't see. Besides, if I do it, it'll show her how brave I am.

I reach down into the hole, but I immediately feel a maze of spider webs. I jerk my hand back out. "You were right. Lots of spider webs down there."

"Forget it. There's nothing down there."

"No, just because there are spider webs, it doesn't mean there are any bad spiders. I'm sure I read, or heard, somewhere that very few spiders will bite a human. One thing for sure, I'm not going to leave without finding out if there's anything down there." I carefully reach down into the blackness and feel around.

No spiders. But I do feel something. I think it's a large piece of paper. Is this what Eichner wanted me to get for him? Is it an important document of some kind? I pull it out to show Jill.

"What is it?" she asks.

"Feels like really thick paper. Maybe it's like . . . parchment or something." I hold it up to what little light is left coming through the window at the far end of the attic. "Looks like a . . . a picture . Maybe it's a painting. On canvas maybe."

Jill looks closely at it and nods. "I think you're right. It's a painted picture. Hard to tell of what. Maybe a man walking."

A painting of a man walking? This is what Eichner urgently wanted me to go get for him?

Jill says, "Why would anybody create such an elaborate hiding place for an old painting?"

I say, "It must be valuable."

She frowns. "Maybe. But if it's valuable, why didn't he take it with him? And if it's so special, why isn't it framed?"

I don't have an answer to her questions. None of this makes any sense. If it is a valuable old painting, and if Eichner somehow came into possession of it, why didn't he take it with him. Or just sell it? Maybe he wasn't thinking clearly. Maybe he was having some kind of mental breakdown and got compulsive about creating a secret place to hide it. Then maybe he forgot about it until now when he found out they were going to tear his house down. That thought makes me think about how much Fred would like this, a mystery to solve about a little painting, not much more than twelve or fourteen inches square, hidden in a special long-forgotten hiding place.

Jill waves her hand in front of my face. "Hello in there. You got awful quiet all of a sudden. What are you thinking about?"

"Aw, I don't know. I'm just trying to figure out why Eichner would hide this so well."

"Maybe it's just a family heirloom. Something he's had for a long time."

"Maybe. But why wouldn't he just take it with him?"

She doesn't have an answer to that, so we both just sit there on the floor looking at it. But no matter how much I stare at the painting, I can't figure out why old Eichner would have gone to so much trouble to hide a simple little painting. "Maybe it's *really* old?" I say. "It could be valuable, and he was afraid somebody would steal it at . . . at the place he was going. We need to get a better look at it. Let's take it with us and go somewhere with better light."

"We can go back to the coffee shop."

I pick up the painting and stand up. "Okay, let's get out of here."

As we head for the metal ladder to get down out of the attic, I unbutton my shirt and flatten the painting against my chest, painting side out. Then I button my shirt back up an pat it down flat to be sure nobody will suspect I've got anything hidden under it.

Jill gives me an odd look. "Why did you do that?"

"Uh . . . I'm going to need my hands free when we climb down that metal ladder."

She shrugs and heads for the ladder.

I follow. But then I stop and look back. "Maybe we should move that counter back where it was. To hide the hole in the floor."

"Why? They're going to tear this place down tomorrow anyhow."

She's right. We might as well just leave it where it is.

We climb down, and I hold her up again while she pushes the metal ladder back up into the ceiling. We carefully make our way down the torn-up stairs and go to the front door. But before we go out, I turn to her and point to my chest. "How does it look? Can you tell I've got something hidden under my shirt?"

"Why? There's nobody around out there."

"Well, uh, I'm just being careful. You never know. Don't forget those holes that were chopped into the walls. Maybe this is what they were looking for."

It seems like she doubts what I'm saying, but she doesn't say anything.

As she leads the way out of the house and across the dirt field toward the ravine, I'm wondering why I feel so nervous. Maybe it's because of how dark it's getting. We must have been inside that old house a lot longer than I thought.

We're almost back to the fence when I think I hear a sound behind us. I look back, but even though I can't see much in the growing darkness, I'm sure I saw some kind of movement back there near the house.

I grab Jill's arm and whisper, "I think there's somebody behind us."

She also looks back, and it seems as if she's going to dismiss it as my imagination, but now I see him more clearly: some guy is coming after us, and it's not surprising that he was hard to see; he's dressed entirely in black.

I whisper to Jill, "We've got to get out of here. Fast!"

She immediately breaks into a full run, and I follow her as fast as I can, but when I look back, I see the man in black is also running, and he's gaining on us. He must be wearing some kind of soft running shoes because he's not making a sound as he runs. What the hell is going on here? Is he the night watchmen? But if so, why isn't he yelling at us to stop?

Jill is a fast runner, and I try to keep up with her, but the torn-up ground is rough, and there are rocks and pieces of splintered wood all over the place. A couple of times I almost fall, and I'm actually surprised that I don't. Every time I look back, I see that the man in black is still gaining on us. I try to tell myself there's no real reason to be scared; he probably just wants us off the property. But I'm not having much luck convincing myself. It isn't just that he's chasing us, it's how he's dressed, all in black, and how he's running, fast and almost silent. Who is he? Is he the one who chopped the holes in the walls of Eichner's house?

Somehow, we make it under the fence and down into the ravine before he catches us. Jill is still moving fast, expertly leading me through the heavy underbrush. Even in the darkness, she seems to know exactly when to go straight ahead and when to turn. It's like she's memorized where every bush and bramble is.

We continue to dodge through the underbrush, maintaining almost a full run despite the darkness, and for the first time, I hear a voice from behind us. He's cursing. Maybe he fell, or got caught up in the brambles.

We make it up out of the ravine and run all the way back to the coffee shop. When I look back, there's no sign of the man in black. He must still be fighting his way through the brambles down in that ravine.

Jill unlocks the coffee shop door and we duck inside.

I whisper, "Don't turn on the lights."

We hunker down behind the counter, and it isn't long before we hear voices outside. Who is it? Is it the man who chased us? Has he now been joined by somebody else? Flashlights slash across the ceiling. They must be looking in through the front window.

The voices finally move away. They sound irritated.

I whisper, "Who was that guy who chased us? Some kind of weird night watchman all dressed in black?"

She shakes her head. "I don't know who he was. Never seen him before."

"You know, Jill, I have the feeling he might have been looking for the same thing we were."

"Really? You think he chased us just to get that little painting? What the heck is it? Let's look at it."

"Well, we don't want to turn on the lights. Somebody is out there. Do you have a back room or something?"

"Only a storeroom."

"Okay. Let's look at the painting in there. Let's crawl and stay low behind the counter."

Jill leads the way as we crawl to a door. She opens it just enough for us to slip inside. As soon as she closes the door, it's pitch black.

She whispers, "I think Granddad has a flashlight in here somewhere.

I hear her rummaging around until a flashlight clicks on.

I see we're in a small storeroom with shelves along both walls. I say, "Did you lock the front door?"

"Yes. But why are we whispering? They're gone."

"Maybe. Maybe not. It could still be that guy who chased us. And somebody else."

Jill doesn't look happy. "This is getting weird, Scott. And now we've led them to Granddad's coffee shop. What if they come back later?"

"Yeah," I say. "We need to stay hidden. For now."

Jill says, "Well, if we're stuck in here for a while, we might as well get a better look at that painting. Maybe we can figure out what this is all about."

I pull the painting out of my shirt, and we sit cross-legged on the floor while she shines the flashlight on the painting. It looks kind of dirty, but it's kind of a nice painting. A man in a straw hat walking out in nature. I say, "Now that I get a good look at it, this whole deal makes even less sense. Could this little painting really be all that valuable."

"It is small, but what if the painter was really famous?" She leans forward to look at it more closely. "I think it's an oil painting, and whoever the painter was, they sure had a steady hand. In art class in high school, they taught us that it's hard to be precise with oil paints. But look how the details of the man's face are nothing more than a couple of dobs of dark red and off-white paint, and yet it works."

"Yeah. Those few daubs of paint makes it look like his face is tanned. And you know what, Jill, somehow that little bit of paint on his face manages to make him seem happy, or at least satisfied. Like he enjoys being out there all alone in nature."

Jill says, "I like it. It's a cool little painting."

I agree with her. Even though the little paining is kind of dirty, it sort of brings the scene to life.

We continue to stare at the painting until Jill finally says, "Well, now that we found it, what are we going to do with it?"

"Actually, Jill, I guess it belongs to old man Eichner. It was his house."

"Did he tell you why he hid the painting up in that attic?"

"He didn't even tell me what it was. He just said he wanted me to go get something for him."

She looks up and shines the flashlight on my face, "And you did it? Why didn't you at least ask him what it was?"

The bright flashlight in my face makes me feel like I'm being interrogated. I push it away and say, "Well, it's kind of complicated. I'll explain it to you later."

"Are you sure it really was his house?"

I shrug. "He said it was his house. And he wrote the address on that piece of paper I showed you."

"Maybe he did own it, but he doesn't now. The county did eminent domain to take the whole neighborhood. That means they paid the homeowners off, right? So now the county owns that house. "

"So, you're saying the county might own this painting?"

"No, my granddad said they only bought the land and the houses. The owners were supposed to come and get everything they wanted. Maybe that means the county owns whatever the owners left."

"And then they hired workers to come in and tear down the houses?"

"No," she says, "they contracted it out to a salvage company. Wait a minute. That reminds me of something the workers told me. They said their boss won the contract to tear it all down and haul it away by underbidding everybody else. The other bidders bid hundreds of thousands of dollars to do the demolition, but their boss said he would do it for free. Just for the salvage rights. To sell whatever they could get out of there."

I think about the implications of what she's saying. "Does that mean the salvage company now owns this painting?"

"Naw, they're just looking for scrap mental and stuff, not things inside the houses. I bet we can keep it. You know, finders keepers."

"Well, don't forget I know who owned that house. Old man Eichner. I think I'd better just take it back to him."

"But don't you think we should try to find out more about it first? If it really is a valuable old painting, I'd sure like to know what it is."

I think about that. "Well, I don't know anybody who might know about old paintings. I do know a schoolteacher. At the mental hospital where I'm working right now. I could ask him."

She nods. "Why don't you do that. Then come back here tomorrow and tell me what you find out. Do that before you give it to old man Eichner, okay? I'm suspicious."

"About what?"

"It just doesn't make sense that he'd hide a valuable painting up in that attic. Maybe he stole it in the first place."

Maybe she's right. Maybe it is something Eichner stole. Does that mean we could keep it? I'm still spooked by that guy dressed in black that chased us. I don't want anybody chasing me from now on. Who knows what he might do. I'd probably be a lot better off if I just give the painting to Eichner and be done with it. On the other hand, I wouldn't mind spending some time with Jill, so I guess it wouldn't hurt anything to hang onto the painting for one more day before I give it to Eichner. I say, "I guess I could do that, Jill. Okay, I'll find out what I can and meet you back here tomorrow."

"Good. But don't come here at the lunch hour. That's the only time anybody is here. The demolition workers, like I said."

I carefully put the painting back under my shirt, and we creep out of the storeroom. I cross to the front window and peek out. No sign of anybody out there. But what if somebody is still lurking about out there in the darkness? Trying to be logical, it seems like they can't do anything to us now that we're out of that fenced-in property. But what if that's not why he was chasing us? What if somebody really is after the painting? If we're going to go outside, I should keep it hidden under my shirt and act innocent.

I open the door and lean out, ready to slam the door back shut if I see any movement out there in the dark. But nobody is there.

I turn back to Jill and whisper, "I think the coast is clear. Let's go quick."

She comes out and locks the door behind her. She starts to head away from me down the sidewalk, but I catch up with her and say, "No, Jill. You'd better let me drive you home. That guy who chased us might still be around here somewhere."

"It's only a few blocks, Scott. I walk home from here every night."

"Please. I'd feel better if you'd let me drive you."

She finally agrees, and we head for my car. Actually, I'm relieved to see it's still in the parking lot.

But then I have to laugh at myself: who would want to steal my old Chevy? This whole episode seems to have made me a bit paranoid, and I don't want to start feeling like that.

We get in the car, and she gives me directions to her house.

When we arrive, she starts to get out of the car, but then she hesitates. "Uh, thanks, Scott."

"You mean for maybe getting you in trouble?"

She does a little laugh. "No, for solving my boredom. Thanks for that. And I'm going to be really curious about what you find out about that little painting."

"Yeah, me too. I . . . well, that is, I mean I wasn't all that bored but . . . well, you know what I mean. I'm curious about the painting too."

She takes a piece of paper and a pencil out of her pocket. "Here, let me give you my home phone number. If you find out anything before tomorrow, give me a call." She writes her number on the paper, and then she does something completely unexpected—she leans toward me and gives me a little kiss, right on my lips.

I do a little laugh, and then I say, "Well, uh, thanks." Then, I realize that must have sounded weird, so I add, "For that kiss, I mean." But as soon as I said it, I wish I'd of just kept quiet.

She gets out, waves goodbye, and heads for the house. It's a small house, painted white with a tidy little grass-covered front yard.

As I drive away, I realize I don't know a thing about her, except that she works in a coffee shop that's owned by her grandfather. I don't even know her last name. When we get together tomorrow, I'd better try to find out more. I carefully fold up the little piece of paper with her number on it and put it into my pocket.

Thirteen

I'm halfway home when I realize that although it's getting dark, it's still early. Why not show the painting to Fred tonight? I'd sure like to know what he thinks of it. But then, I don't know where he lives. I wonder if I go back to the hospital, somebody there might know where he lives. The hospital is not far, and I've got nothing else to do tonight, so it's worth a try.

I pull into the parking lot and park in my usual place. I'm the only car in the visitor lot, but there are several cars in the employee lot. I guess that makes sense; there must be a night shift.

Before I go in, I put on my sports coat with my student visitor badge still pinned to it.

I'm still feeling a bit spooked about that guy who chased us after we left Eichner's house, so I look around before I get out of my car. Nobody in sight. Why am I feeling so nervous? This is where I normally park, and I never felt worried before.

Okay, time to go. I smooth down the front of my shirt to make sure nobody can tell I've got something hidden under it. I get out of the car and hurry toward the administration building.

Once I'm inside, I'm a bit surprised to see the same gray-haired guard lady sitting at the entry desk. She's reading a book. I think it's a romance novel. It's not all that late, but it is dark outside, and I saw her here this morning. She must work pretty long hours.

I point to my student visitor badge and explain to her that I'm supposed to meet my friend, Fred the schoolteacher, but I don't know where he lives.

With her eyes still on her book, she uses her thumb to point to the nearby hallway. "Room eight," she says. Fred is still here at this time of night? And would he be here in this administration building?

I go down that hallway until I find room eight. I tap on the door. Immediately, I hear Fred yell to come on in.

I go in and find him sitting on a couch eating something. He has a large white box on his lap, and he's watching a small TV. The only other furniture in the room is a narrow bed that's sagging in the middle. No kitchen. Not even a fridge.

With his eyes still on the TV, Fred says, "Hey, Scotty. What're you doing here?"

"Hi Fred. Uh, you live here?"

He chuckles. "Of course I live here. Me and the foreign doctors trying to get U.S. credentials all have rooms in this building. You don't think I'd be working at a crap job like this unless they gave me free room and board, do you? The cheapskates only give me the one lunchtime meal a day, but this room is free. And the nice guard lady at the front desk has a phone, so I can use it to order in food. Hey, sit for a spell and talk to me. Want a donut?"

I tell him no thanks, but he opens the large white box anyhow and says, "All I got is jelly-filled. With them, you get the most for your money."

I sit down on the couch next to him. "Listen, Fred, I need to ask you about something. You remember I told you old man Eichner wanted me to get something for him from his house? Well, I did it."

Fred stops his next donut halfway to his mouth. "What? You said you'd take me with you. So we could look for clues. To look for the old lady's bones and stuff."

"There are no clues there anymore, Fred. No bones. In fact, there's nothing there. They're tearing out the whole neighborhood. Putting in a big new shopping center. I was just going to drive by and take a look at Eichner's house, but I found out right away why Eichner said he didn't have much time left. His house is about to be torn down."

"Really? They're ripping out all the houses?"

"Yeah. I met this girl who told me all about it. She—"

Fred's eyebrows go up. "A girl? You met a girl? Your age?"

"Yeah. Her name is Jill, and she works in a coffee shop right across the street. She told me—"

"Is she cute?"

"Well, yeah, but the important thing is she knew all about the neighborhood they're tearing down because she grew up nearby. She said it was called War Town because it was developed during the war. World War Two. A big war munitions factory was there, and so they built houses for the workers. Anyhow, she said she could get me inside the fence, so I did it."

I pause my story, and Fred shows his impatience by shaking his donut at me. "Well, go on. Did you find Eichner's house?"

"Yes, I did. But the strangest thing is that it was the only house still standing."

"What? Why would his house be the only one not torn down? But get to the important part. Were there any bones in the back-yard? Were the cops there?"

"Jeez, Fred. Slow down. One question at a time. There were no cops there. Nobody was there. It was a demolition zone. Behind a tall chain-link fence. And no, there weren't any bones in the backyard because there wasn't a backyard anymore. Every-thing had been all plowed under by big bulldozers. Nothing was left anywhere but torn-up dirt and debris, the remains of all the houses they'd knocked down. Eichner's house is the only one left because he's fighting it. In court, I mean."

"Fighting it in court? What does that mean?"

"He's saying the house should be protected as a historical building."

"Wait a minute? You're saying Eichner, the old guy locked up over there at Cottage H, is fighting some kind of court action? How could he be doing that from here?"

"I wondered the same thing, Fred. But maybe it's not him doing it. Maybe somebody else is trying to keep the house stand-ing. While we were inside his house looking for Eichner's secret hiding place, I got the feeling somebody else was looking for the painting. There were holes in the walls, and after it got dark, some guy chased us away."

Fred holds up one hand. "Hold up a second, Scotty. You lost me. What holes in what walls? Somebody chased you? And what was that about a painting?"

"Big holes somebody chopped in the walls of Eichner's old house. Like they were looking for something hidden. But never mind about that, the painting is what's important. I found it hidden in Eichner's attic. It's what I came here tonight to tell you about. Check this out." I pull the little painting out of my shirt and smooth it out on the sofa between us.

Fred leans forward to carefully look it over. "It's not very big."

"Right, but it's the thing that was hidden in the secret place Eichner told me about."

Fred wipes his hands on his pants and picks up the painting. "Looks old." He examines it closely. "It's kind of cool though. I can see why old man Eichner would like it."

"Yeah, for such a little painting, it's kind of interesting how nice it is. Captivating, I think. Jill liked it too. But let's think about this, Fred. You said you like a mystery. Why did Eichner hide this little painting at his house? Why didn't he take it with him? Why did he go to all the trouble to make a secret hiding place for it in his attic?"

Fred breaks into a grin. "Great! A mystery. Now the fun begins." He puts the painting back down on the couch and taps it. "I bet it has something to do with him killing his neighbor lady."

"I thought about that too, but I can't see how it could be related. But even if it was, it still doesn't explain why he didn't take it with him. It was obviously important to him."

Fred thinks about that for a few moments, then says, "I bet he had to go on the run. That's why he couldn't take it with him."

"On the run?"

"Yeah. I bet he was running from the cops. After he killed his neighbor lady."

"But he said he got away with that by feeding her body to his dog."

"As if we can believe anything he says."

"True. But look at it, Fred. It's only a little painting. If he was on the run, he could have taken it with him. I've been carrying it around inside my shirt. He could have done that too. No, there has to be another explanation about why he left it. Why he hid it in his attic."

Fred runs his finger along the edges of the painting. "Look at this, Scotty. Uneven edges. All the way around."

"Yeah, I noticed that. Don't all paintings on canvas have edges like that?"

"Not like this. It's been cut. All the way around. Like with a knife." He snaps his fingers. "I have it. It was cut out of a frame."

"Cut out? Why? If he liked his painting so much, why would he do that?"

"He must have been in a hurry."

"But he took time to create a special hiding place for it. Under the floor up in his attic."

"Then it was cut out of its frame sometime before."

Fred stares at me, and I think he has the same idea I have. We both say it at the same time: "He stole it."

Fred grins. "That's it. By God, Scotty, we figured it out. The edges are cut because he stole it. He must have gone into some museum and cut it right out of its frame."

"So you think this is actually a valuable painting? Wait a minute, Fred. I've been in museums. They have guards all over the place."

"Yeah, but only during the day. A slippery character like Eichner could've broken into the museum at night to grab this little painting. Think about it. A guy who'd kill his neighbor lady? It doesn't seem like much of a stretch for him to get into stealing paintings. When he was younger, I mean."

We both stare at the little painting, and I try to imagine it as something valuable, something that was in a museum. That makes me look at it in a different way. It is small, but it's pretty nice, even as dirty as it is.

"You know Fred, if this could be a valuable painting, something stolen from a museum, I'd better try to find out more about it before I give it back to Eichner. Maybe one of the art professors at the university can tell me about it." I pick up the painting and stand up.

Fred doesn't get up, but he does reach up to shake my hand. "Great. Do that and come back tomorrow and tell me what you found out. This mystery is getting really good."

"Well, I have classes tomorrow, but I'll try to drop by later in the day."

"Make sure you do. I won't be able to concentrate at all tomorrow. We've gotta solve this new mystery."

I turn down his final offer of a jelly-filled donut and let myself out. Out in the hallway, I stop to look one more time at the painting. What if Fred is right? What if it really is a valuable old painting, something stolen from a museum? I again hide it inside of my shirt. Then, I hurry out of the building and run to my car as fast as I can.

On my way home, I keep thinking about what Fred said. Could Eichner really have stolen the little painting from a museum? And what does that say about Eichner? Could he be a lot more than the old man mental patient he appears to be?

When I get home to my little apartment, I hurry inside and lock the door. But now I'm not so sure I should have done that. What if somebody is hiding in here waiting for me?

But then I realize I'm just being paranoid: nobody can hide in a one-room apartment.

Just to be sure, I check inside the bathroom.

Nobody in there either.

But the door to the little cabinet under the sink is slightly open. Did I leave it open? I don't remember doing that, but I guess I might have.

I look around the entire apartment, trying to tell if anything else has been disturbed. My psych textbooks from the library are stacked on the floor next to the wide couch that also serves as my bed. Did I leave my books stacked up like that? Seems like they were spread out a little more. And the library book I was reading is on the bottom of the stack. Wouldn't it still be on top?

I shake off those kinds of paranoid thoughts. It's just that it's been a crazy day. I must be getting jumpy and imaging things. Nobody has been in here looking around. There's no way anybody could know I was at Eichner's house today, and even if they did, there's no way they could know where I live.

I take the painting out of my shirt and put it on the counter that separates the kitchen area from the rest of the room. I turn on the overhead light to get a better look at it.

It really is a cool little painting. Maybe I should just put it on my wall and not tell anybody where it came from. Nobody is ever likely to come here to visit me. Nobody ever has. After two years at the university, I haven't gotten to know a single one of the other students.

What about Jill? Would she want to come visit me sometime? Not likely. She's got her own life to deal with. A coffee shop to run and a grandfather with big plans for it.

But she did say she wanted to know what I find out about the painting. And she did give me her phone number. And what about that goodnight kiss? Maybe we'll get to know each other better. Maybe a lot better.

I decide to focus on that thought and stop thinking about the painting.

Tomorrow will be another big day, what with classes and maybe a visit to the university art department to talk to an art professor. I'd better try to get some sleep.

Fourteen

I wake up thinking that if I get to campus early, I might be able to find a professor in the art department who can tell me about the painting. I again hide it inside my shirt and go out, locking the door behind me. For some reason, I'm still feeling a little paranoid, so I look around to see if anyone is watching me. There's no one around except for the little dried-up foreign-looking lady who seems to spend all her time outside of her apartment sweeping the sidewalk. Is she a cleanliness freak, or does she do that in order to keep an eye on everyone? She doesn't seem to notice me passing by her, so I don't bother to say anything to her on my way to my car.

I arrive at campus early, and not many student are around, so I'm able to get a close-in parking place. As I pass the central fountain, there are only a few anti-war protesters there. They're are huddled together, probably planning the days protest activities, so for a change, they don't bother me. Hurrying through the all-but-deserted campus, it doesn't take me long to get to the art department building. The faculty index is next to the elevator, and it says most of the professor's offices are on the third floor. I take the elevator up there.

This early in the day, the third floor hallway is empty. But then, a young guy comes around the corner. He's dressed in white coveralls covered with smudges of paint. He must be a painting student. I catch up with him and ask him which art professor might know about the history of oil paintings. He says there is only one professor of art history in the department, Professor Bauer. He points out where that professor's office is, at the end of the hall.

When I get to that office, the door is closed, but there's a note indicating his office hours are later in the morning. I'll have to come back then to talk to him.

It's still too early to go to my clinical practices class, but I've got nothing else to do, so I head for the psychology building.

This time, when I get to the empty classroom, I don't sit in the back. I take a seat very close to where Professor Spence is going to be seated.

But then, I change my mind and get up and move back a few seats. No use letting the other students think I'm trying too hard to be noticed. After all, I'm only a brand new psych major, and because this is a 400-level course, the other students have probably already taken a lot of other psych classes. But even if there are advanced students in the class, I think I can keep up. And maybe they'll be more likely to accept me if I tell them about what I'm learning at the hospital.

The other students straggle in, chatting together. As before, they don't talk to me. I wonder what they'd think if they knew what I have under my shirt and the story behind it.

Professor Spence arrives right on time and closes the classroom door. After he's seated and looking over his lecture notes, two more students arrive. As they're trying to quietly close the door, the professor turns to look at them. He says, "I'd appreciate it if you'd all arrive here on time. If the door had a lock on it, I'd lock it at the exact time the class is supposed to start."

The two late students mumble something about the anti-war demonstrations, but the professor ignores their explanation and begins his lecture. He says, "Some of their so-called treatments were both unscientific and horrific. For example, at one time, many doctors believed that all mental illness was caused by syphilis. Just to prove it, they went so far as to intentionally infect subjects with syphilis. Sure enough, when the syphilis got advanced enough, the subjects began to show deviant behavior. But eventually, the doctors found that a lot of their mental patients didn't have syphilis, so they decided there must be more than one kind of mental illness. They began to study the brain itself, digging into the brains of mental patients after they'd died. They tried to find specific physical malformations in the brain to account for specific types of deviant behavior. When the brains of mental patients didn't show any significant differences from the brains of normal people, a variety of other approaches were tried. All of them failed and were abandoned."

He pauses to look at us. I keep on writing to show him how diligent I am at taking copious notes.

Then, he continues, speaking in a clear, if passionless, voice: "Back in the 18th century, when religion was a key component of daily life, many felt mental illness was a moral issue. Mental patients were therefore treated by trying to instill moral discipline in them. Often that involved simply talking to them about their mistaken behavior. That eventually led to the so-called talk therapies and other modern psychoanalytic approaches."

The professor goes on to say that over the years, many new treatments were tried, and many of them did serious harm to the patients, both physical and mental. He describes the common use of straight jackets to calm disruptive patients and such radical treatments as forced vomiting, raising blisters on the skin with boiling water, and of course, the old Civil War-era standby, bleeding. He says, "Of course, none of those treatments worked either, but throughout history, doctors have felt they had to at least try something rather than doing nothing at all. That led to some odd-ball theories such as phrenology, the belief that bumps on a person's skull might indicate hidden mental problem in the brain. In fact, there was a period in which mental health doctors routinely began ordering dental work to be done on patients because they believed mental problems indicated that unseen tooth infections had moved from the mouth to the nearby brain. When removing bad-looking teeth didn't work, they resorted to pulling out all the patients' teeth."

Like all the other students in the class, I'm still taking notes, but that last one makes me look up at the professor to see if he's trying to make us feel disgusted at such barbaric treatments. However, he appears to be merely reading from his notes, not taking any position on the rightness or wrongness of such misguided theories. He goes on to say that when removing a patient's teeth didn't work, the doctors of the time didn't want to give up on their theory that mental illness was caused by tooth infections. "Instead," he says, "they just modified their theories. They decided that infections elsewhere in the body must be causing the mental problems. Therefore, they tried removing any part of the body that might be harboring infections. Over the years, they tried removing tonsils, appendixes, thyroid glands, and gallbladders."

For the other students in the class, this might be old stuff, but I'm finding it really interesting. As this point, the professor pauses to look at us again, and I realize I'm now the only student not taking notes. I quickly go back to writing in my notepad.

He goes on: "Eventually, they had to give up on the infection theory, so they tried going the other direction, infecting the patients with diseases to see what would happen. For example, they infected a number of patients with malaria. Although such treatments were causing the death of many patients, they were so sure they were on the right track, they published what they said was promising results. In 1927, the Nobel Prize committee awarded the prize in medicine to practitioners of the alternative disease approach. Later, an even more radical treatment, lobotomy, which involves the severing of connections in the brain's prefrontal cortex, also won the Nobel Prize for medicine."

As the professor pauses to look at his notes, I decide it's time for me to do what I'd planned. I raise my hand and say, "Excuse me, Professor Spence, what about shock treatment?"

He looks at me for a long moment before he says, "That type of treatment should be referred to as electroconvulsive therapy. They began using it in the 1930s, for various mental conditions. I'll be getting to that."

"Oh," I say. "Okay."

I guess I shouldn't have interrupted him. I should have realized he intentionally hasn't been pausing to let anybody ask questions, and none of the other students had been speaking up. I guess that's just not his teaching style. I hope he doesn't resent my interrupting him and give me a bad grade. I push that thought away. Maybe it's only that none of the other students have the kind of direct experience I have, and that's why they haven't been speaking up.

The professor starts to go on, but then, he seems to change his mind. "Since we have a question on the floor about the convulsive therapies, I might as well summarize that topic now. It started many years ago with chemically-induced seizures. Some doctors reasoned that because mental illness was rare in epileptics, the seizures were somehow protecting their brains. They tried numerous seizure-inducing drugs, including strychnine and massive doses of caffeine. Eventually, they settled on metrazol, a chemical that stimulates the circulatory and respiratory systems. They reported great success with a number of patients, but it was dangerous. The seizures sometimes caused physical injuries, and it often resulted in a compete loss of memory. Eventually, they found a quicker way to induce the seizures, by delivering electric shock to the brain using electrode pads placed on either side of the head."

He pauses to look at me. "And to answer your question, yes, it is still used today, mainly for serious, long-lasting depression. But it is also experimentally being used to find out if it helps with other type of serious mental illness. The procedure itself has been much improved since the early days. Now, the procedure is done under general anesthetic. In other words, the patients are asleep. And they are given a muscle relaxant to avoid injury. The patient does not actually experience the shock-induced seizure. In fact, because the patient is under general anesthetic, a blood pressure cuff has to be attached to the patient's ankle, to stop the muscle relaxant medication from entering the foot and affecting the muscles there. That way, the doctors can watch the movement of the patient's foot to be sure a seizure is actually taking place."

The professor looks directly at me and says, "Does that answer your question?"

I hesitate, and then say, "Uh, yes, but—"

Another student, a young man with a budding beard, interrupts me, saying, "Yeah, but does it work?"

The professor stares at him for a moment, and then says, "The answer to that question is a bit complicated and somewhat controversial. I'm planning to discuss the efficacy of such treatment methods in a later lecture."

I raise my hand again to bring his attention back to me. "What I was going to ask was what about the after effects? I saw one patient who seemed to be completely out of it afterwards."

Professor Spence stares at me. "You've seen the procedure done?"

"Well, no, but I've seen the guy, an old man, who afterward seemed to have been knocked for a loop . . . Uh, I mean he was really out of it. Even a day later."

The student with the half-beard is looking at me. "You work in a mental hospital or something?"

"Well, I'm not exactly working there. I signed up for the three credit hours. The one-semester experience there."

Another student pipes up: "You're getting credit for working there? Why didn't we hear about that?"

Professor Spence holds up one hand to stop the discussion. "It was something arranged through the department and the local mental hospital. On a trial basis. They decided to allow one student to come in for one semester. It was . . . " He takes a piece of paper out of his pocket. "Scott here who was the first student to sign up. Maybe next semester there will be opportunities for others. Depending on how it goes."

The other students stare at me and grumble a bit under their breaths. I'm pretty sure they're wondering why a "newby" in the psych department got such a plum opportunity. Now they'll probably hate me, but it's not my fault. I quickly say, "I didn't know it was an unusual opportunity. I just saw the notice on the bulletin board, so I went in and applied."

The other students don't seem to be satisfied, but the professor again looks at me and says, "That's all right, Scott. Why don't you tell us about this old man you've been observing."

Now everybody is waiting for me to explain. How much should I tell them about Eichner and his weird story about killing his neighbor? But as soon as I have that thought, I realize I shouldn't do that. Then I might have to also tell them about his talking me into going to his house where I found the painting. I say, "This is a clinical practices course, so I guess you want to hear about the kind of treatments I'm seeing at the hospital. The problem is I haven't really seen any clinical practices. Mostly the old men just sit around and do nothing." I stop. Should I tell them about the terrible things Fat Freddy, the schoolteacher told me? No, I didn't actually see them.

Professor Spence saves me. "Just tell us about what you've observed. I mean with regard to electroconvulsive therapy."

"Well, there's this old man on the ward I've been assigned to. They sent him out for electroconvulsive therapy even though he didn't seem depressed or anything. At least he didn't seem depressed to me. He, uh, just likes to talk. That's all."

Professor Spence says, "It's hard to imagine why they would assign him to electroconvulsive treatment unless he was suffering from severe depression. Perhaps he has mood swings. Have you noticed anything like that?"

I'm not sure how to answer that question. It doesn't seem to me like old man Eichner is the type to have mood swings, but maybe I don't really know what that is. I decide to answer honestly. "Well, I might not know what that is. And maybe I haven't been there long enough . . . I mean, haven't seen enough of him to be able to tell."

The professor smiles. "All right. Then, that's your assignment. You will observe and report back to us next week. We should take full advantage of this opportunity the university has given you. You can give us a weekly report on current treatment practices at our local mental institution. All right?"

I quickly say, "Oh, sure. The old men on my ward don't do very much, but I'll report whatever I see."

The professor says, "Good. And with that, I think we'd better get back to our discussion about beliefs that led to more modern theories of mental health treatment."

He goes back to lecturing, and I'm taking notes, but I'm having a hard time concentrating. His words seem to support my theory that they gave Eichner the shock treatment as punishment. According to Professor Spence, Eichner is not they type of depressed patient that would normally qualify for shock treatment. Actually, Eichner seems like the most normal person on the ward, except for his weird story about killing his neighbor.

After Professor Spence finishes his lecture and dismisses the class, I hurry out of the room without talking to any of the other students. I don't want them to start asking me a bunch of questions about what the mental hospital is like, and besides, I want to get back to the art department to see if I can find out more about the painting.

Fifteen

I hurry across campus to the art building and take the elevator up to the third floor. I go straight to Professor Bauer's office. I tap on his door, but there's no answer. The note on his door says he should be having his office hours right now, but it's obvious he's not here. I'm ready to give up and come back later, when a short gray-haired man wearing a rumpled suit comes out of the elevator. Is that him?

Sure enough, he comes straight toward me, and before he even gets to me, he says, "If you're trying to get into my art history class, it's too late. The class is full."

"No," I say quickly, "If you're Professor Bauer, I wanted to talk to you about . . . something else."

"Oh," he says. "What is it?"

I look down the hallway. There doesn't seem to be anybody else around right now, but I'd rather not pull the little painting out of my shirt here in the hallway. "Uh, can't we go inside your office? It's about . . . well, can't we just talk about it in your office?"

He looks at me strangely, but he does unlock the door. We go into the very small, very cluttered office, and he points to the chair in front of his desk.

While he takes off his suit jacket with his back to me, I quickly pull the little painting out of my shirt and place it on his desk. "My name is Scott. I'm a student here. Not an art student though. Psychology. Anyway, I wanted to ask you about this painting. I was hoping you could help me. I mean . . . uh, tell me about it."

He takes off his glasses and picks the painting up. He looks at it, and then he puts his glasses back on and looks at it even more closely.

Does he recognize it? I'm getting so excited I can't contain my curiosity. "Uh, what do you think? I mean, maybe it could be a real old painting, couldn't it? By a famous painter. Or something."

He puts the painting down on his desk and says, "No, I don't recognize it. But I do recognize the style. I think it's a copy of a van Gogh."

"Oh yes," I say, "I think I've heard of him. He was pretty famous, wasn't he?"

He glances at me and then smiles as if I'd said something funny. "Yes, he was. In fact, he's one of the world's most famous oil painters. He was a plein-air artist. That means he painted outdoor scenes. Back in the 1880's. This must be a student copy of one of his works. Maybe the original is in a museum somewhere. Let's see if I can find it in one of my books." He stands up and goes to his floor-to-ceiling bookshelf.

I have to admit I'm kind of disappointed. A student copy? But what if he's wrong? It looks really old. Maybe it's not just a copy.

I tell myself not to get carried away. Professor Bauer said it was only a copy, so it probably is. What did I think? That I had a painting by one of the world's most famous artists stuffed down inside my shirt?

"Ah, here it is," he says. "It's called *The Painter on the Road to Tarascon*." He turns the book around so I can see.

I'm amazed at what he's showing me: it's a picture of my painting. Now I'm really excited. My painting really is famous. It's even in a book.

"It says the Nazis placed it in a museum in Magdeburg, Germany. But it got destroyed during the war when the allies bombed that town."

His words bring me down fast. It's as if he played a trick on me, telling me I had a famous painting, and then he pulled the rug out from under me. I point at my painting that's still lying on his desk. "So this is uh, not the real painting? "

He picks it up again and stares at it for a moment. "No. But it looks old, so it's possible it was made back then. When it was in that museum. Where did you get it?"

"Oh, well, I sort of . . . found it."

"Found it?"

"Yeah. I was rooting around in an old building that was being torn down."

"I guess that makes sense. Now that it's in van Gogh books, copies of it are undoubtedly being made and sold commercially."

"Uh, are you sure this is only a copy?"

He takes off his glasses and smiles at me again. "What did you think?" That you found an original van Gogh that would be worth millions."

"Millions? Uh, well, I didn't know anything about it. I just thought . . . well, that it looked old."

He puts on his glasses and again looks closely at it. "Yes, it does look old. But maybe that's just because it's dirty. It needs to be cleaned."

"So you don't think it's valuable?"

"Not really, even though it's a damn good copy. Looks to me like whoever made the copy had studied van Gogh's techniques. Even got the brush strokes just right. But look at the uneven edges. It's been trimmed. Maybe to fit into a smaller frame or something."

"I thought maybe that meant it had been cut out of a frame."

He looks a bit startled. "You mean you thought it was stolen?"

"Yeah."

"Not likely a copy of an old painting would be stolen, but who knows. Like I said, it could be an old student copy made from the original while it was still in that German museum. But that would have been a risky thing for a student to do back then. Van Gogh was one of the painters Hitler had declared degenerate. Hitler had such paintings placed in museums simply to show his people what degenerate art looked like."

I point at the painting and say, "So somebody must have made a copy way back then. It's in your book."

"True. We do know what it looked like, so obviously some-body did make a copy before it was destroyed during the war. Maybe an art student just liked it and made his own private copy.

Or maybe it was an art class assignment back then. Maybe in defiance of Hitler. Who knows?"

"So this copy might be that old. Made before the war. Wouldn't that make it valuable?"

"If it was copied from the original, that might make it a little more valuable. As a historical piece. If you want to leave it with me, I can try to do a little more research on it."

"Uh, no. I think I'll just hang onto it. Or maybe I can sell it. I sure could use the money."

"Oh, I wouldn't sell it if I was you. It's a nice little painting. You could clean it up a bit and put it on your wall."

"Clean it? How?"

"Oh, there are professional art cleaners, but they're expensive. Not worth the expense in this case. But you can do it yourself."

"I can? How?"

"Believe it or not, some professional oil painting restorers sometimes clean parts of paintings by using q-tips and their own spit."

"Really? Spit?"

"Yeah. You might be able to clean it up a bit. It's worth a try. You can buy a box of Q-tips at any drugstore. Make sure your mouth is clean and put the Q-tips in your mouth to get it wet. But not too wet. Then start cleaning small areas. Try it, and see how it goes. Use a fresh Q-tip often."

"Uh, won't it take off any of the paint?"

"Not likely, but you'll find out quick. If this really is a painting done by a German student back in Germany before the war, the paint will be fully hardened by now. But start up on one corner, just in case it's the work of a more modern student."

I pick up the painting and stand up. "Well, thank you."

"No," he says, "thank *you*. For letting me look at what might be a piece of history. That is, assuming this copy was done by a student all those years ago. It's a shame the original got destroyed by the allied bombing, but that was war. A lot of art got destroyed in Germany during that war."

I walk back down the hallway to the elevator, thinking about what Professor Bauer told me. At first, I was excited that my painting was in a book, and that it was done by a really famous artist. But then, when I found out it was only a student copy, I felt tricked.

That gives me another thought. What if Eichner got tricked too. What if somebody convinced him it was a real van Gogh, and he paid a lot of money for it? That would explain why he wants to get it back so bad.

As I walk to the elevator, I'm starting to feel worried again. If anybody else sees it, they might also think it's an original painting done by that van Gogh guy and try to steal it from me. After all, Professor Bauer said the original would be worth millions. I put it back inside my shirt to hide it.

I hate to do it, but I decide to skip my afternoon class. There's just too much going on. As I head back across campus to get to my car, I keep looking back to see if anybody is following me. Doesn't look like it. But why would they? I'm getting all nervous for nothing.

Sixteen

I get into my car and head for the hospital. I don't want to go to Cottage H, but I do want to tell Fred what I found out about the painting.

But then, I realize Fred will be in his classroom teaching. I'll have to wait and go there later. I pull over to the curb to think about what I should do next.

I know, I should go tell Jill what I found out. She said I shouldn't come back to the coffee shop at noontime because that's when all the workers come in, but it's a little past noon now, so hopefully the workers will be gone.

I drive to the coffee shop, and I'm disappointed to find that it's closed. I get out of my car and check the listed hours on the front door. It says it should still be open. I look through the coffee shop's front window, but there's nobody in there. I rap on the door to make sure she's just not in the storeroom, but there's no answer.

I turn away and look across the street to the demolition site. There's quite a bit of activity over there, with heavy equipment still involved in pushing the debris from the demolished homes up into big piles that are then being loaded into dump trucks and hauled away. In the distance, I see that Eichner's old house is still standing. That's a surprise. Jill seemed pretty sure they were going to tear it down today. Early this morning in fact. Maybe Eichner managed to keep his legal restraining order in place. That's assuming it was him that filed it.

I go to the fence and manage to get the attention of one of the demolition workers. When he comes over to the fence, I say, "Hi. I'm a friend of Jill's." I point toward the coffee shop. "She told me yesterday that they'd have finished tearing down all the houses by today, but I see one of them is still standing."

He turns to glance at Eichner's house. "Yeah, damn it. That's the last house to go. It was scheduled for today, but then the inspector did a walk through, and guess what they found. A dead body."

I stare at him, not quite sure what he means. Could he be referring to Eichner's old neighbor lady. Did they find her bones? "Do you mean like . . . like a skeleton or something?"

"Naw. A regular dead body. Some old guy got killed in that house last night. Who knows why. The cops were crawling all over it this morning. After they took the body away, the cops said the house is now a crime scene, and we can't tear it down yet."

He starts to walk away, but I call him back. "Uh, did the cops say what happened? I mean was it like a murder or something?"

"Yeah, a murder. That's all they told us. Hey, I got to get back to work now."

"Okay. Thanks. Uh, by the way, did Jill say why she was closing early today?"

"She never opened this morning, so we had to go somewhere else for lunch today." He walks away.

I stay by the fence, watching the heavy equipment move the remains of the destroyed houses into big piles. A murder in Eichner's house? What the hell? And he said the police think it happened last night. It must have been after we left. Did it have something to do with that man that chased us. Maybe he caught somebody else in the house last night. Somebody also looking for the painting. Does it mean that he would they have killed us if he'd caught us? This whole thing is getting damn scary, and it makes me very aware of the painting that's hidden inside my shirt. I hurry to my car and drive away as fast as I can.

I'm again heading for the hospital, but all of a sudden, I get worried about Jill. I'd better go by her house to tell her about the murder. I can also tell her what I found out about the painting, and we can talk about if maybe the murder in Eichner's house might have something to do with the painting.

I drive to her house, but it has that empty feel houses have when nobody's home. But I should make sure. I park in front of her house and go to knock on the front door.

Nobody comes to the door, and there's not a sound coming from inside.

I go around to the back and look in through the window. Nobody in there, and no lights on.

All of a sudden, I get worried. What if somebody sees what I'm doing? What if somebody is watching her house?

Now why did I have that thought? Did hearing about that murder in Eichner's old house make me start feeling paranoid?

I go back to my car and drive away quick. I still have her phone number in my pocket. I'll call her from my apartment.

I'm only a few blocks from home when the paranoid feeling comes back, and I pull over again: what if somebody is waiting for me at my apartment? If they want the painting bad enough to have killed somebody for it, I'd better not go anywhere they might be able to find me.

But that's not logical. There's no reason anybody could know where I live, or that I have the painting. That man who chased us last night couldn't have known who I was. It was dark.

For sure, I should hide the painting somewhere in my apartment and quit carrying it around with me. I start driving again, but the closer I get to my apartment, the more nervous I feel. Where in my apartment could I hide it? If someone came there looking for it, really searching for it, there's absolutely no place in my little apartment I could hide it where they wouldn't easily find it.

Maybe I should just take the damn painting straight to Eichner and be done with it.

I pull over next to the lake to think about it. Some kayakers are out there paddling along next to each other. Are they racing? Soon even more kayakers come, but they're staying close to each other, talking. Not a race. Must just be some kind of big kayak outing.

I notice the sun reflecting off of the water. It's getting low in the sky. Jeez, how long have I been parked here watching the kayakers? Am I trying not to think about that dead man they found in Eichner's old house? The truth is I don't have any idea about what to do next.

But Fred always seems to know what to do, and he should be off work by now. I'll go to his room and tell him what I learned about the painting and about the dead body. Maybe he'll have some ideas about what might be going on and what I should do next.

Seventeen

At the hospital, I park and hurry into the administration building. I tell the guard lady at the front desk I'm going to Fred's room to talk to him about something. I think she probably knows me by now, but I point to my student visitor badge anyhow, and she waves me by.

I knock on Fred's door, and just like the last time, he immediately says to come on in. I wish he would stop doing that. With all that's been going on, he should lock his door until he finds out who's there.

Fred is sitting on the couch, exactly where he was sitting the last time I visited him. And he's again eating from a big box of jelly-filled donuts. He holds the box out to me and says, "Hey, Scotty, glad to see ya. Here, have a donut."

I wave off the donuts. "Listen, Fred. Some heavy shit is going down. Remember I told you when Jill and I were leaving Eichner's house last night, somebody chased us. Today I went back out there, and one of the workers told me they found a dead body in that house. Some old guy. Murdered."

Fred halts the donut he was about to put into his mouth and stares at me with his mouth still open. "Somebody got murdered? In Eichner's old house?"

"Yes. And I bet it has something to do with the painting, don't you think?"

Fred stares at me, wide-eyed. "Jesus, Scotty, what've you got yourself into?"

"Well, there's no reason for anyone to know I was in that house last night. I mean, yeah, that guy did see Jill and me as we were running away, and he chased us, but it was dark. He couldn't have known who I am."

"Maybe, maybe not. The important thing is what are we gonna to do about it?"

"We?"

"You bet we. You and me. We're gonna go at this like a couple of real sharp detectives and figure it all out. We got ourselves a real live murder mystery now, so we have to solve it. Now, here's what we do. Over there on the table is a yellow pad. Grab it and let's write down the clues."

"I'm not so sure I want to be a detective, Fred. I think I should just give the painting to Eichner and be done with it."

Fred shakes his head and says, "Naw. What would be the fun in that?" He goes back to eating his donut as he thinks. Then, he looks up at me and says, "Okay, here's the way I see it. You were right not to take the painting to Eichner. Either he'll get in trouble because he has it, or else he's in on it."

"In on it?"

"Well, he wanted it bad, didn't he? Maybe he hired somebody to go get it. Killers."

"Aw, I don't know, Fred. Eichner is just an old man in a mental hospital. What would he have to do with any killers?"

Fred finishes his donut and grabs another one out of the box. Excited, with his mouth still full of jelly donut, he says, "He may look like an old man, but what do we know about him? We know he killed his neighbor, and we know he somehow got his hands on an old painting. Probably stole it. What does that tell you?"

"Now wait a minute, Fred. We don't know any of that for sure."

Fred shrugs. "Maybe, or maybe not. But that's how we detectives have to work. We form hypotheses, and then we act on them until we learn otherwise. Now, what did you do with the painting? Did you hide it somewhere?"

"No. I couldn't think of anywhere to hide it at my place." I pull the painting out of my shirt and put it down on the sofa between us.

Fred nods, staring at the painting. "Seems to me you have to hide it. You can't just carry it around with you."

I'm feeling at a loss. It doesn't seem like Fred has any more of an idea of what to do than I do.

Fred says, "Okay, let's think about this. First off, we got ourselves a murder, Eichner's neighbor lady. Then he sends you to find this painting. The question is, what do the two things have to do with each other?"

"I don't know, Fred. The supposed murder of his neighbor lady was a long time ago. How could that have anything to do with this painting?"

"Oh, but it does. Or at least maybe it does. A good detective never believes in coincidences. We can't overlooks any clues."

"Right now, I'm more worried about somebody finding out I have the damn thing. It seems like somebody is willing to kill to get it."

"So, you think we should destroy it? Throw it away or something?"

I look at the little painting. It's beautiful, in its own way. Then I realize I forgot to tell Fred what it is. "Oh, no. We can't do that. It's a famous painting."

"It's what?"

"I mean it's a copy of a famous painting by an old time painter named van Gogh."

"Are you kidding me, Scotty?" He again taps the painting. "This little thing is a van Gogh?"

"Yeah. I forgot to tell you. I went to see this art professor. At the university. He looked it up in one of his books and found out it used to be in a German museum. But he said the original got destroyed during the war, so this has to be a copy."

Fred wipes his hands carefully and picks up the painting. He looks at it very closely. "How about that. A van Gogh painting. I thought it looked pretty darn good."

I nod. "Yeah. Too bad it's only a copy."

Fred is still staring at the painting. Then, he looks up at me. "And you believed that so-called art professor? I bet he tried to get you to give it to him, didn't he?"

"Well, yes. He said he could keep it for a while and do more research on it. But only to find out if maybe it was a copy made way back then. Before the war."

Fred shakes his head. "I don't believe him. I think this is it. The original. I think Eichner stole it. Just look at the edges. I told you it was cut out of a frame in a museum. Eichner is a German, right? And he's old, old enough to have been in Germany during the war. I bet he stole it from that museum a long time ago, back when he was in Germany, and he's kept it hidden all this time."

I stare at the painting, thinking about how carefully it was hidden in a specially-built place in Eichner's attic. And there were lots of spider webs down in that secret hole. That means he hid it there many years ago. "But the art professor said the original would be worth a lot of money. Why wouldn't he have put it in a safe deposit box or something?"

Fred shakes his head. "Not if he lived through the destruction of his entire country. Nothing survived in Germany, especially not banks."

I'm wondering if Fred could be right. Old Eichner certainly is secretive. Maybe he doesn't trust anybody, not even banks. But why did he trust me? What is it about me that made him decide I was the one to go retrieve the painting for him? "I don't know, Fred. Why would he choose me, a student that he hardly knows to go get it for him?"

"Who's better? If you don't mind me saying it, Scotty, you're kind of a naive young fellow. Or maybe I should say an honest young fellow. Straightforward. Anybody else he chose would probably just steal the painting and get rich off of it. But not you. Even now, you want to take it to him, don't you?"

"Sure I want to take it to him. Especially if it really is valuable. Anything to get it out of my hands. Are you forgetting somebody may have got themselves killed because of this little painting?"

"I'm not forgetting that. It's what made me realize it's not a copy. It has be the real deal. Didn't you say that art professor said it was worth millions? People will kill for that kind of money. Besides, it's too late now to give it back to Eichner. Now that you showed it to that art professor, he knows it exists. You said he's an expert. He wanted you to give it to him. That means he knows it's not a copy, and now he knows who has it. I think you're in danger, Scotty. Real danger."

I can't believe what he's saying. I'm in real danger? How in the hell did I get myself mixed up in this? Why did I let Eichner talk me into going to his house in the first place? Maybe it's partly Fred's fault, convincing me to play detective. Even after that guy chased Jill and me, I still didn't get smart enough to just take the damn painting back to Eichner and be done with it. Was I showing off to Jill? And where is she? I hope none of this has anything to do with her disappearance.

Fred opens his box of donuts and carefully chooses one. He uses the donut to point at me. "Got you thinking, didn't I?"

He sure did get me thinking. Just a few days ago, I was just an undergraduate student with no friends. And before that, I figured there was a good chance my draft lottery number would get drawn and my main worry would be about how to keep myself from getting killed over there in Vietnam. Now look at me. I'm in even more danger right here in my own home town. And the more I think about it, the more I realize there's no way out of this. I can't stop thinking about that guy in black that chased Jill and me. If I take the painting to Eichner, that guy might figure out who I am and come to Cottage H. Then not only will I be in trouble, Eichner will be in trouble too. In fact, everybody at Cottage H could be in danger.

Fred is finishing his donut, so he opens the big white box to take out another one. He holds the box out to me. "Sure you don't want one?"

"Damn it, Fred, no, I don't want a donut. Will you stop eating long enough to help me figure this out?"

He puts the donut back in the box, but not before taking a big bite of it. He grins at me, his teeth completely covered with red jelly donut. "Got to eat to keep the old brain working good, don't I?"

I shake my head in frustration. I can't believe Fred is taking this so casually.

"Okay, I have it," he says. "You have to hide it here. Here in my place. I've got twenty-four hour security right at the end of my hallway. Anybody coming here would have to get by her. Any strangers start hanging around, they'd stand out like a sore thumb." He holds up a fat thumb to make his point.

I look around his room. It's even smaller than my little studio apartment. "Hide it here? Where?"

"I got me a perfect hiding place. Grab the painting and come with me. I'll show you." He manages to heave himself up off of his couch and leads me toward the back of the room. He wants me to leave the painting with him? Am I sure I want to do this?

There I go again, wanting to get rid of the damn thing, but at the same time, not wanting to let it out of my hands. But I feel like I can trust Fred, and besides, he's right: he's got 24-hour security, so it's better to hide it here than at my place.

Fred leads me into his tiny bathroom. "Watch this," he says. He grabs the sides of the white metal medicine cabinet that's above the sink and yanks the whole thing right out of the wall. "Discovered it a while back. One day I opened the door too fast and found out the whole thing was just stuck into the wall. Nothing but a little bit of glue holding it. I got it completely loose, and now I use it to hide my emergency rations." He points to a very large candy bar that's leaning against the back of the hole.

"So we should just stick the painting in there with your candy bar? What if the chocolate melts and gets on the painting?"

"Good point. We should wrap the painting in newspaper first." He hurries out of the room and comes back with a page of the city newspaper.

I carefully wrap the painting in the newspaper and put it behind the big candy bar. Then Fred carefully pushes the cabinet back into the wall. "See there," he says. "Nobody would ever suspect."

He's got a point. If anybody did manage to get past the guard, they'd never guess the medicine cabinet can be removed from the wall. And why would they think Fred had anything to do with it in the first place? Even if somebody did follow me to the hospital, once I was inside, they couldn't know where I went.

Fred is grinning. "Told ya my brain works good when it's well fed, Now, how about that donut?"

I realize I haven't thought for one moment about eating today, so I decide to accept Fred's offer of a donut.

As soon as I've finished the sweet and sticky donut, I tell Fred I've got to get home to get some studying done. I say, "I'll meet you in the cafeteria tomorrow. We can talk more then, okay?"

"Okay, buddy," he says. "Hey, we've got a real mystery goin' now don't we? Fun, eh?"

"Yeah, real fun," I say. "Maybe fun enough to get me killed."

Eighteen

I head for my apartment, but halfway there I change my mind. I do need to get some studying done, but right now that doesn't seem as important as trying to find out why Jill has disappeared. I turn around and head for her cafe.

I park my car in front of the cafe, but I can already tell it's still closed. I get out and look across the street. Eichner's house still hasn't been torn down, and two cops are there on the front porch of the old house talking to some of the workers. One of the workers points in my direction and the two cops look my way. Are they pointing at me? No, more likely they are just pointing at the cafe. But why? I decide there's no reason for me to hang around if the cafe is still closed, so I might as well drive by Jill's house again to see if she's there.

I start my car and head that way, but I don't even make it a block before I see red lights in my rear view mirror. For just a moment, I think about not stopping, but then I decide they probably just want me to pull over so they can get around me.

But no, as soon as I pull over, the cops pull up right behind me. Why are they stopping me? Are these the same cops that I just saw talking to the demolition workers?

Both of the cops get out of their car and come toward me, one on each side of my car. The cop on my side of the car taps on my window, so I roll it down, and that's when I notice he has his gun out. Thankfully, he's not pointing it at me as he says, "Show me your license and registration."

"Sure," I say. I quickly get out my license and registration and hand it to him.

As he's looking at it, I say, "What's the trouble, officer? I don't think I was speeding or anything."

He stares at me for a long moment, and then, thankfully, he puts his gun back into its holster. "No, you're not speeding. We just need to talk for a few minutes." The cop writes something down in a small notebook and hands me back my license and registration.

The other cop goes back to their police car, and I can see he's talking on their police radio. Is he calling in my license plate number? But why? Are cops suspicious of all young men? Maybe because of all the anti-war demonstrations? Or is it something about me?

The cop opens my car door and says, "Why don't you get out of the car, son."

I get out, and he leads me around to the front of my car. He's closely inspecting it.

I say, "What are you looking for? Can I help?"

"Just making sure there's no damage. Tell me, son. Is this the only car you have access to?"

"Yes. Actually, this old Chevy is the only car I've ever had. My mother bought it for me. To go to school in. I'm a college student. At the university."

"A college student, eh? Well, the university is a long ways from here, isn't it, son? So why are you hanging around here? We asked the workers back there if they'd seen anybody hanging around, and they pointed you out."

I smile, making sure to act completely open and friendly. "Oh that," I say. "The cafe back there. Across the street from them." I point in that direction. "My girlfriend works there. Her name is Jill. But she hasn't opened it up for some reason. I just came by to see if she's back."

He seems to relax. Maybe the workers told them I'd only been hanging around the cafe.

He says, "Here's the deal, son. We found a dead body in an old house back there in War Town. An old man. At first we thought . . . well, never mind what we thought, but eventually the coroner told us the guy hadn't been killed in that house. He'd been hit by a car somewhere else and brought there. He had headlight glass imbedded in his forehead."

I know immediately what it means: somebody is going to great lengths to make sure that house doesn't get torn down. They placed a dead body there to make the house a crime scene. So it wasn't murder. Or was it? Did somebody nearby get intentionally run over? And how did they get the body into the demolition area? Do they have a key to the gate? "Brought there?" I ask. "Why would anybody do that?"

"That's what we're trying to figure out, son. But your car doesn't have any front end damage, and it doesn't look like you've replaced either one of your headlights."

"No, sir. Never have."

He stares at me, and then he looks down at his little notebook. "That address on your license current?"

"Yes, sir. That's my apartment. Near the university."

"Okay, well, we may want to talk to you some more later. Okay?"

"Sure. No problem."

He starts to walk back to his police car, and I think about asking him if he has any idea of why Jill hasn't been opening her cafe.

No, there's no reason he would know anything about that.

As soon as the cops turn their car around and head back toward the demolition site, I get back in my car and head for Jill's house.

But once again, there's no sign she's been there, so I head for my apartment.

By the time I get back home, I'm feeling a little less nervous. The painting is well hidden in Fred's bathroom.

I park my car in front of my apartment, but I don't get out until I'm sure nobody followed me. Still, it's completely dark now, so if anybody was following me. I'd have seen their car lights. But just to be extra careful, I stay in my car for several minutes until I'm sure nobody else is around. No one is, except, of course, for the little dried-up foreign woman who's outside, as always, compulsively sweeping the sidewalk.

I get out of my car and nod to her as I pass.

As she sweeps, she does her usual weird mumbling to herself and doesn't even seem to notice me.

The first thing I do once I get inside and lock my door is look around to see if anything has been moved. After carefully checking, I'm sure everything is exactly as I left it, because this time, I'd made sure to memorize where everything was. I even stacked my textbooks in a certain order, and in a slightly off balance stack, to make sure I'd know if they'd been touched.

Next, I go to the phone and call the phone number Jill gave me. I let it ring for a long time, but no one answers. I hang up and check my watch. It's not all that late. Maybe she just took her granddad out to a movie or something. I decide I'd better get some studying done and call her later.

I pick up one of my library books and sit down. I try to focus, but with everything that's been happening, I'm having trouble concentrating. I catch myself reading the same paragraph over and over again. It's about the brain's phospholipid bilayer being made up of two layers of lipid molecules. What does it matter if such lipid molecules are flat and that they form a continuous barrier around brain cells? What matters is that Jill might be in trouble.

I wake up with the textbook on my chest. I didn't want to fall asleep, but I guess I was worn out.

But what time is it? I glance at my watch and see that it's after midnight. Now it's too late to call Jill.

Or is it? If they went out to a movie or something, maybe they just got home, and she'll still be awake. Even if she's asleep, I bet she'd still want to hear what I found out about the painting. And maybe she hasn't even heard about the dead body they found in Eichner's old house.

I decide to call her, but as before, her phone just rings and rings. Why would she and her granddad be out so late? I decide to keep on calling her, all night if necessary, until somebody answers the phone.

I go back to reading, but I stop every half hour or so to call her number.

Finally, the clock says it's getting close to dawn, and there's still no answer. Obviously, nobody is there. Could they have gone out of town or something? If so, it wasn't planned; she said she wanted me to come back to the cafe to tell her what I found out about the painting. And besides, wouldn't she have left a note at the cafe to tell the workers the cafe was going to be closed for a while?

But maybe I'm getting all upset about nothing. When I find her, I'm sure she'll have a logical explanation about why she had to go away for a while. At least I hope so.

Nineteen

By the time I wake up, it's almost noon. I kept on trying to call Jill until almost dawn, and then I must have fallen asleep reading. I'd better hurry to the hospital to tell Fred what's going on.

I drive to the hospital and hurry to the cafeteria. It's open and full of employees, but Fred isn't there. How can that be? I can't imagine Fred missing a meal. Maybe he got held up with his teaching. I'm hungry, but I decide I'd better go to his classroom to tell him I can't find Jill. On my first day, the nurse that showed me around said I was free to walk around the grounds, as long as I didn't go into any of the other wards or into any of the treatment buildings. Fred's classroom building can't be considered to be a ward, so there's no reason I can't go there to talk to him.

I go to the classroom building, but when I get there, the door is locked, and there's no sound coming from inside. That's odd. As far as I know, Fred teaches every day. Remembering all those jelly donuts he was eating last night, and that warning he got from his doctor that he was going to eat himself to death, I get worried. Maybe he's sick and all alone in his room with nobody to help him.

I hurry to the administration building and tell the usual guard lady at the front desk I'm going down the hall to see Fred.

She waves me by.

I knock on Fred's door, but there's no response. I try the door handle and discover it's unlocked. I open it a crack and call out, "Fred, are you here?"

There's no answer, so I go on in. He's not in bed, which is a relief. But could he be passed out in his bathroom? A quick check in there tells me he's not anywhere in his little apartment. And he isn't at his classroom teaching, so where could he be?

Then, I have a scary thought. What if the killers came here and took him away. Did they force him to tell where the painting is hidden?

The medicine cabinet seems undisturbed, but just in case, I pull it out of the wall enough to see behind it; the painting is still there, as is his big "emergency" bar of chocolate.

I push the cabinet back into the wall and go back out into his room to think. When I told the guard lady at the desk I was going to see Fred, she seemed to think he should be at home. Why wouldn't she know he was gone? Maybe if he left in the middle of the night. I hope that's all it is. But where did he go?

I should just go to Cottage H and talk to Eichner, and then I'll come back here later. Fred will probably be back by then.

I hurry to Cottage H and force my way past the Scribbler. Of course that sets him off writing a flurry of imaginary notes. As I head for Mrs. Grimm's desk to check in, I notice Eichner is not sitting on his usual bench. I sure hope they didn't send him out for more shock treatment just because he talked to me again.

Before I even get to Mrs. Grimm's desk, she stands up and says, "Oh, there you are."

"Uh, I had a long night of studying. Did you need me here for something?"

"Well, no, but Mr. Grimm wants to talk to you. Go ahead and knock on his door."

I go to the door to Mr. Grimm's apartment, but before knocking, I hesitate. Why would he want to talk to me? Did I do something wrong?

No, stop that. It's just my imagination acting up again. That dead body at Eichner's old house, and both Jill and Fred being missing has got me worrying about everything.

Well, only one way to find out what Mr. Grimm wants. I knock on the door.

Almost immediately, I hear his voice say come on in, Scott."

How did he know it was me? Did he tell his wife to send me in as soon as I arrived? Or maybe somebody called him to tell him I was wandering around the grounds.

Mr. Grimm is waiting for me in the doorway to their apartment. He says, "Come into my office for a moment, Scott.

He doesn't seem any more friendly than Mrs. Grimm was.

He leads me through to his office and gestures for me to sit in the chair in front of his desk.

I decide to remain standing.

He also stays where he is, standing behind his desk, staring at me.

"What?" I say.

"Tell me something, Scott. Do you happen to have an idea of where we might find Mr. Eichner?"

"What? Is he gone? I noticed he wasn't sitting at his usual place."

I have the strong feeling Mr. Grimm doesn't believe me.

But then, he seems to change his mind. "No, it's all right. It's just that Mr. Eichner seems to have disappeared. He somehow got past the Scribbler in the middle of the night."

Got past the Scribbler in the middle of the night? Would it be all that hard to get past that frail old man? "Uh," I say, "does the Scribbler stay by the front door all night?"

Mr. Grimm waves that question off and says, "Never mind that right now. The point is, Mr. Eichner seems to have somehow disappeared. The grounds have been searched, and he's nowhere to be found. The reason I wanted to talk to you is because you seem to be the last one he talked to. Did he say anything about leaving? Do you have any idea where he might have gone?"

"Me? No, I don't know. Why would I?"

Mr. Grimm pauses before he says, "Well, all right, son. It's only that it's something of a mystery. This has never happened before. These old men don't just get up and leave. Not on my ward anyhow. You may go now, but if you hear any of the other patients talking about how or why he left, be sure to come and let me know."

"Oh, sure. I will." I start to leave, but then I remember those two men. I turn back. "Uh, maybe it has something to do with those two men I saw talking to Eichner in the dorm."

"Two men? They were talking to Eichner in the dorm?"

"Yes, two men in suits. Younger men. I'd never seen them before."

Mr. Grimm looks at me for a long moment before he says, "I'm sure you must be mistaken, Scott. I never heard about any visitors coming onto the ward recently. It must have been two of the other patients. Maybe you can look around and tell me if you remember which two they were."

I'm ready to protest and tell him I'm sure it wasn't any of the other patients, but he dismisses me as if he doesn't want to hear any more about it."

I leave their apartment, and as I pass Mrs. Grimm's desk, she says, "Everything all right?"

"Apparently, it's not. He told me Mr. Eichner has disappeared. How could that have happened?"

"Well, we'll figure it out, Scott. Don't worry about it."

As I walk the ward, I'm trying to figure out why Eichner would have run off. When I didn't come back to the ward right away, did he give up on me going to his house to retrieve the painting and decide to go get it himself? If that's what he did, he probably won't be able to get through the demolition fence. On the other hand, if he could prove it's his house, maybe they'd have to let him in. But even if he somehow did get in, it could be very dangerous for him. After all, there's already been one dead body found in that old house.

Wait a minute! What if the dead body found in the house was Eichner? The police said the body was an old man that had been run over by a car. But why would they kill Eichner by running over him with a car? That doesn't make sense. If they were after the painting, wouldn't they just force him to tell them where is was hidden? And they wouldn't run over him with a car. That wouldn't get them anything.

As I walk past Eichner's bench, I'm wondering why Mr. Grimm would think I'd know where Eichner went? Had Eichner been talking to him about me? No, that's not likely. But maybe Mr. Grimm has been getting reports about me talking to Eichner from some of the other patients. And why did Mr. Grimm doubt my story about the two men I'd seen talking to Eichner in the dorm? I described them as younger men wearing suits. It doesn't seem likely those two men could have gotten onto the ward without him knowing about it. Somebody besides me must have seen them.

After walking the ward for a while with nothing happening, I decide there's too much going on out there in the real world to be hanging around here. I tell Mrs. Grimm that I have to go because I've got some studying to do. Which is true. But of course, I'm not going to go study right now; I've got to find out what happened to Jill. And Fred. And Eichner.

Twenty

I hurry to the administration building to again look for Fred, but the guard lady at the front desk is only willing to interrupt her romance novel long enough to tell me Fred hasn't returned to his room yet. I ask her if anybody else has been there asking about him.

Without looking up from her book, she just shakes her head.

"No strangers?"

This time she does look up from her book. "Strangers? What do you mean?"

"I mean has anybody you don't know come here asking about Fred?"

"Nobody comes here. Strangers or otherwise. The foreign doctors go by me on the way to their rooms, but they hardly seem to notice me. You're about the only one who comes in by the front door. Everybody else parks in the employees lot, and then they go right to their building."

I thank her and head for my car. Where the heck could Fred have gone? And why didn't the guard lady know he was gone until I told her? Did she take a break, maybe to go the restroom or something, and Fred got out without being seen? But why would he sneak out? He told me he never goes anywhere. He even orders his food brought in. And if he did leave, where would he go? Could be possibly have gone to the demolition area to try to get into Eichner's house? Is he out there somewhere trying to solve the mystery by himself?

I start my car, but I just sit there wondering where I should go. To Jill's house? To the cafe?

Yes, that's it. I should go back to the cafe. Maybe Jill's back there. That would be a relief.

As I pull out of the parking lot, I feel something pressing against the back of my neck. It feels like cold metal.

"Just keep driving. I have a gun. I will tell you where to go."

What the hell? Is it the killer? How did he find me? Wait a minute, I know that voice. "Is that you, Mr. Eichner? What are you up to?"

"Just remain quiet and keep driving."

"Sure. But why would you need a gun to talk to me? Aren't I still your friend?"

"I thought you were, but you did not do what I told you to do. You said you would help me. You said you would go to my house before it's too late, and—"

I pull over to the curb. "You don't really have a gun, do you, Mr. Eichner?"

"Where would I get a gun? It is only a little piece of pipe I found. But I do need your help. Please."

I turn to face him. "Well, Mr. Eichner. Maybe I'll help you. But I need to know more. First, I want you to come around and get in the front seat here next to me. Then we can talk."

Eichner sheepishly slips out of the car and gets into the front seat. I see that he's wearing black pants and a white shirt, just like the kind of "uniform" the hospital employees wear. Did he steal those clothes? And he's wearing shoes. Where did he get shoes?

"All right now," I say, "what's this all about? Why are you escaping from the ward?"

"I am not escaping. I entered that institution voluntarily. I am supposed to be able to leave anytime I want to, but Mr. Grimm won't let me out. He's an evil man, Scott. You need to watch out for him."

Mr. Grimm evil? I look into Eichner's eyes. He seems to really believe what he's saying. And there's another thing in his eyes: he's scared. I haven't even seen him look scared. I should probably turn around and take him right back to the hospital, but something about the urgency of his words makes me unsure. "Now wait a minute, Mr. Eichner, if you're a voluntary patient, why would Mr. Grimm be keeping you from leaving?"

"Because he wants to sell me to the Israelis."

The Israelis? I'm beginning to think old man Eichner is getting paranoid. Maybe that's why he's in a mental hospital. But I haven't seen any other evidence that he thinks people are after him. "Israelis? What Israelis, Mr. Eichner?"

He hesitates for a long moment, and then he says, "Let me explain the whole thing to you, son. It all goes back to Germany. To my home town, a place called Magdeburg. Do you know of it?"

So, he really is from Magdeburg, the town that had the museum where the painting was displayed. If I can keep him talking, he may reveal that the little painting is a genuine van Gogh. "Magdeburg? Uh, yes, I think I might have heard of it."

"Of course you would have heard of it. You are a university student. Magdeburg is where the Russian and American Army came together at the end of the war. And that is part of my story. I grew up in that town, and during the war I was working as a guard in the town museum. And that is the problem. Being a guard, I mean. The Israelis think I was a guard in the German government prison camp there. But that camp was across the river. I didn't have anything to do with it. There were stories about what was being done to prisoners in that camp, but none of us in the town really knew. A cousin of mine, also named Eichner, was a guard in that camp, but I only met him once, when I was a mere child. I tried to explain that to the Israelis. I told them that it was my cousin that worked in that prison camp, not me. They did not believe me. They accused me of killing many Jewish people. But that is not true. I did not know anything about that."

"Now wait a minute, Mr. Eichner. You say you've talked to the Israelis. When was that?"

"Just recently. In fact, you saw them. In the dorm. Mr. Grimm gave them a key to the back door, and they keep on coming in to threaten me. They say they are going to get proof that I was a guard in that camp, and then they will come back to arrest me. They say they will take me to Israel to stand trial."

"So, you say you were a guard in a museum, not in the German concentration camp. Does you being a guard in a museum have something to do with what you wanted me to get from your house?"

Eichner just stares at me. Is he going to suddenly clam up just when I'm about to find out if the painting is a real van Gogh?

Finally, he says, "You want to know about my job in the museum? Why do you want to know about that?"

"Uh, just curious."

For several moments, he just stares at me. Then, he says, "You found the painting, didn't you? You went into my house and found it."

I have to keep him talking. Better to keep him guessing. "What painting are you talking about, Mr. Eichner?"

He again pauses for what seems like a long time, but then, he seems to make up his mind. "I will tell you what happened, son. One night the Americans bombed my city. The people who operated the museum knew it was coming, so I was given the job of moving all the paintings and other historical artifacts down into the basement. I took them all down there for safe keeping, but I made sure I put a wonderful little painting by a Dutchman named van Gogh in an especially safe place. I loved that painting. There was not a time that I walked through that part of the museum that I did not stop to look at it. And when students were allowed in to make copies of it, I kept a close eye on them to make sure they did not touch it. On the night of the bombing, I hoped the painting would be safe down there. But the bombing was too terrible. The museum was on fire. The whole town was on fire. It was horrible. You cannot imagine. Hiding down there in that basement with all the paintings, I was barely able to breath because of all the smoke. I knew I had to escape. I cut that painting out of its frame, and I hid it under my shirt. I ran."

So, it's just as I expected. It really is the original van Gogh painting. Eichner stole it from that museum. Having carried the little painting around for days inside my shirt, I could easily imagine Eichner doing the same thing as he ran from the falling bombs. "So you stole the painting. It's not really yours."

"It does belong to me. It belongs to me as much as anybody. If it was not for me, it would have been destroyed by the bombing. Burned by the fire that burned down the entire museum."

Eichner holds out both of his hands, as if he's begging me to believe him. I do believe his story about stealing the painting from that museum, but whether he did it during the bombing is questionable. He may have stolen the painting as soon as he heard there was going to be a bombing. Or, if the painting was safe in the museum basement as he says, he could have taken it while the bombing was creating chaos. He could have even burned down the museum himself to cover the theft. Maybe he took a lot of paintings, and the van Gogh is the only one left. Maybe he sold the others to get the money to build his big fancy house. Where else would a museum guard get the money to come to this country and build himself such a nice house? I decide against admitting I have the painting. "That's quite a story, Mr. Eichner. But you're wrong about me having it. How could I have it? Listen, I'll take you to your house. You'll see that it's too late. The whole area is fenced off, and your house is ready to be torn down."

He looks confused and . . . frightened? Is he afraid he's lost the painting forever? Or is he afraid that I'm going to turn him in to the Israelis? I decide the best thing to do is what I said. I'll take him to his old neighborhood, and he'll see that his house is gone. Or if they haven't torn it down yet, he'll see that the whole area is fenced off, so there's no way I could have gotten in there.

Eichner is silent as I drive. I wonder if he's thinking he's already told me too much.

When we get there, I'm disappointed to see that the cafe is still closed, and across the street, even though the heavy equipment is continuing the demolition process, Eichner's house is still standing.

He points and says, "See there, my house is still there." He turns back to look at me. "You said it was torn down."

"Well, they said it was about to be torn down. All the others have been."

Eichner gets out of the car.

"Wait," I yell. "Where do you think you're going? I have to take you back to the hospital."

"No," he says over his shoulder as he walks toward the fence. "I have to get in there. It is as I told you. The painting is up in the attic of my house." He hurries toward the fence.

I start to get out of the car and chase him down, but no, he won't be able to get past that tall fence. And even if he talks to the workers, they'll tell him his house is now a crime scene, and he can't go in. I'm better off out of it. He says he's a voluntary patient. If so, it means he can leave the hospital if he wants to, and I guess it also means he can also go back to the hospital if he wants to. After all, as far as I know, he has no place else to go.

Right now, my main concern is for Jill. I'll drive to her house and hopefully, she'll be back from wherever she and her granddad went. But when I get to Jill's house, it looks as vacant as ever. But just in case, I again knock on both the front door and the back door. I look in all the windows, hoping the neighbors don't call the cops. But inside, everything is the same as the last time I was here. Not only are they still gone, it doesn't look like they've been back at all.

Where could they have gone? Try as I might, I can't shake the worrisome feeling that Jill's disappearance must be because we found the painting. Could that guy in black that chased us have somehow found out where she lived? Did he kidnap her and her grandfather to try to find out where the painting is? I sure hope not. She'd probably have to tell him that I have it, if for no other reason than to protect her grandfather.

I get back in my car and just sit there wondering if I should call the police. But what would I tell them? That my girlfriend— no, actually a girl I just met—isn't home. They'd think I was crazy.

Twenty-One

Today is the first meeting of my Human Cognition class. The professor is lecturing about the philosophical antecedents of psychology, talking about rationalism versus empiricism. I am interested, but I can't stop thinking about where Jill and Fred might have gone, and why they both disappeared at the same time. Talk about human cognition: my cognition wants to see a connection between the disappearances of my only two friends, even though there's no reason they should be related. Unless, that is, both disappearances are related to the painting. And what about Eichner? Could he have something to do with them disappearing?

The professor is saying Plato, a rationalist, believed that the route to knowledge is through thinking and logical analysis. But Aristotle, an empiricist, believed that we acquire knowledge via empirical evidence; in other words, through experience and observation.

His words make me realize I must be more of a rationalist, always thinking about what is or what could be.

Okay, what is? Jill and I found an old painting in Eichner's house that Professor Bauer, an art professor who specializes in art history, thinks is a student copy of a lost van Gogh. But now Eichner tells me that it really is an original van Gogh that he removed from an art museum in Germany in order to save it. And I can't stop relating it to that guy in black that chased us. How does he fit in? And what about the dead body they found in Eichner's house? Was that only to keep the house from being torn down, or is it also related to somebody wanting the painting? And does any of it really connect to the disappearance of Jill and Fred? All the things that have happened must be related in some way. They can't all be coincidence. But might it all be just false connections that my brain is making up?

Now, the professor is talking about perception. He's saying perception is altered by how the perceiver tends to see things; in other words, we see what we want to see. I have the weird feeling that he's talking directly to me. He's suggesting that what I believe is going on with all these mysteries is only what I want to think is going on, that it's my brain making false connections. But can that possibly be true? Am I making up relationships where they don't exist? Causes and effects that aren't really there? I've been thinking that everything that's happened to me is related to Eichner and the painting. In fact, I'm doing it right now, barely hearing the lecture, and instead thinking about holes chopped in walls, a little van Gogh painting, some guy in black that chased us, and both Jill and Fred disappearing at the same time. But what if none of those things have anything to do with one another? What if my brain is doing what the professor is lecturing about, making connections where they don't really exist?

For some reason, the professor has abruptly switched to talking about structuralism. Or did I space out and miss something he said to make the connection? He's saying a structuralist, when perceiving a flower, would analyze it in terms of its size, geometric form, constituent colors, and so on. But, he says, such things can also be analyzed through introspection, taking the information we perceive and thinking not about those factors but instead thinking about how our minds are deconstructing what we are perceiving.

It hits me that given what the professor is saying, I have to reanalyze everything. I have to determine how much of it is being created by my own mind.

I jump out of my seat and head for the door. The professor stops talking and stares at me, and so do all the other students.

As I run out the door and down the hallway, I realize I'll have to apologize to that professor later for disrupting his lecture. But maybe he'll understand when I tell him that I realized how important what he was saying was.

I run all the way to my car and get into the back seat. I lie down on my back, trying to catch my breath. I stare up at the car's interior ceiling and try to think it all through logically. Why did Eichner tell me that story about killing his neighbor when I first met him? It must have been a test to see how I'd react. Maybe he was just looking for someone he could talk into going to his house to get the painting, someone he could trust not to steal it. I must have passed his test. Eichner probably sized me up as a loner. All the better for him. But then Jill helped me find the painting. Eichner didn't figure on that. I was ready to bring the painting to him as soon as I found it, but Jill talked me out of it, at least until we could find out more about it. And Fred also talked me into keeping the painting long enough to do more research about it. He didn't want "the mystery" to end. He wanted to play detective, probably because he was bored. Eichner didn't count on that either.

I sit up and look out the car's front window. It's a nice sunny day, but I don't think it should be. It should be a dark sky, with the kind of clouds that hold the threat of an approaching thunderstorm.

I try to shake such thoughts off. I don't want to get into that kind of negative thinking. I should just focus on the situation, and try to be logical about it. The problem is the painting. It's what is causing all of the problems. But now Eichner's run off, I can't get rid of it by giving it to him. I really like the painting, but if I got rid of it, there'd be no reason for anybody to come after me. And no reason for anybody to hurt Jill or Fred.

Fred thought Professor Bauer knew it was genuine and wanted it for himself. So, maybe that's the solution: I should just give it to him. And when he finds out it's a real van Gogh, he'll have it put in the university art museum. That would be a good place for it. I should go back to Professor Bauer and tell him I found out the painting was saved before that museum was destroyed in the Allied bombing.

I get into the front seat and start the car. I'll go to Fred's room, get the painting, and take it to Professor Bauer right now.

Twenty-Two

Back at the hospital, I go straight to Fred's room, and he's still not there. From the look of his room, I'm pretty sure he hasn't been back at all. I head for his bathroom, but I'm half suspecting the painting will be gone. Maybe it's better that way. If somebody wants it that bad, they can have it.

I tug the medicine cabinet out of the wall, and there it is, right where we left it, still wrapped in newspaper. And Fred's "emergency" candy bar is still there too, virtually proving that Fred hasn't been back.

I unwrap the painting and hide it under my shirt.

I hurry out of the administration building and run to my car.

As I drive away, I get worried that somebody could have seen me running away. There's absolutely no one around, but I can't shake the worried feeling I get every time I have the painting under my shirt.

I drive back to the university, constantly looking in my rear view mirror, making sure no one is following me.

I hurry toward the art building, forgetting to detour around the anti-Vietnam war protesters who are, as usual, gathered around the central fountain. Seeing me, a draft-age male, they immediately start yelling at me with their bullhorns, telling me to join them, telling me to get up on the top step with them and burn my draft card, which of course I'm not going to do, especially not with the plainclothes policemen standing by with their cameras. The last thing I want right now is for them to take notice of me.

At the art building, classes are just letting out, which is good. Nobody will notice one more student in the hallways.

I take the elevator up to the third floor, and thankfully, I see Professor Bauer's office door is open. I hurry to his office and find him at his desk, writing something in a notebook. Is he writing something about me, about the strange student who came to his office to show him a famous van Gogh painting?

No! I've got to stop thinking like that. If I learned anything in that Human Cognition class, it's that everyone thinks the world revolves around them. It doesn't.

I slow my walk as I approach the door to his office, trying to act casual, as if I was in the area and just happened to drop by to see him.

I tap on the side of his doorway to get his attention, and he looks up at me. "Oh, it's you again. I was just thinking about you because I did a lecture this morning about all the wonderful works of art that were lost in the war. The students found my lecture very interesting, especially when I showed them slides of supposedly lost art pieces that are still being found in unexpected places."

Is he implying my painting might actually be an original van Gogh? "So some lost paintings are still being found?"

"Not only paintings, but also sculpture, and things like gold jewelry. Things stolen from the Jews by the Nazis."

"So, my painting could be . . . "

He smiles. "So, you're still hoping that little painting of yours is a genuine van Gogh."

Should I tell him what I found out from Eichner? If I tell him I have new information about where my painting came from, would he take it more seriously? No, I'd better keep that information to myself. Who knows if Eichner is actually telling the truth.

The professor chuckles. "I'll take your thoughtful silence as confirming it. Not so surprising actually. Who wouldn't hope they'd found a real treasure. Well, son, there's only one way to find out. We'd have to do some tests on it."

Can I trust him? Does he really think it's only a copy? "Well, I—"

"Do you have it with you?"

"Sure, I've been . . . well, sort of carrying it around with me."

I pull it out of my shirt, and that makes Professor Bauer chuckle. "Well, that's one way to carry it." He stands up. "Well, come on. Put it back in your shirt if you like holding it so close to yourself, and let's go to the museum. I know a guy there."

The university's art museum building is right next to the art department building, but instead of going up the broad stairs and into the front door, Professor Bauer leads me around to a back door and knocks.

A short heavy-set man opens the door and seems surprised to see us. "Well, well," he says, "if it isn't James Bauer. To what do I owe this pleasure?"

Professor Bauer reaches out and shakes the man's hand. He says, "Nice to see you too, Charlie. It's about a painting, of course. This young man has some questions."

Charlie, invites us in without asking my name. "Excuse the mess," he says, indicating, with a wave of his hand, a long work-bench littered with various bottles of something, paint brushes, and metal tools. A number of framed paintings are leaning against one wall.

Professor Bauer turns to me and says, "Show it to him."

I pull the painting out of my shirt.

Professor Bauer takes it out of my hand and shows it to Charlie. "Recognize it?"

Charlie takes the painting and examines it. "Can't say I do. What is it, a forged old master?"

"I don't think it's a forgery," says Professor Bauer. "I think it's a student copy of a lost van Gogh, but Scott here wants to hope it's genuine."

Charlie grins. "A genuine lost van Gogh? Now wouldn't that be something?"

Professor Bauer is also smiling. "Yeah, how'd you like something like that to walk into your lab? No, it's obviously a student copy. The original was in a museum in Germany. Proba-bly looted from France by the Nazis. It was lost during a bomb-ing in the second world war. The museum was destroyed. But we'd like to find out how old it is. It could be a copy that was made back then, while it was in that museum."

Charlie says, "Well, let's take a look at it." He leads us to his workbench and says, "Too bad it's been cut out of its frame."

He looks at me. "You may not know this, young man, but you can tell a lot about a painting from it's frame. For example, if the framing of the painting was fastened with staples, then we know it was mounted after 1937."

"What about the canvas?" asks Professor Bauer.

"Right," says Charlie, turning the painting over. "Old, I'd say. Yellowed. But hard to tell how old." He turns the painting back over. Done in oils, and obviously dried a long time ago. Let's take a look at it under the scope."

He leads us to what looks sort of like a microscope with two eyepieces that's mounted on his workbench. He slides the painting under the scope and uses it to examine the painting.

Professor Bauer says, "Craquelure. The pattern of cracks in the paint. Different paintings, from different countries, produced at different times have different craquelure patterns."

I nod to show him I understand, even though I don't. "Uh, can that show if it's a real van Gogh?"

"No, but it tells us it's pretty old. There are a lot of fine cracks, but I suspect this painting has been out of it's frame for some time, and it hasn't been handled with care."

Uh oh. I hope my carrying it around inside my shirt hasn't ruined it.

But then, he adds with a smile, "But if it was a genuine van Gogh, I don't supposed anybody would care about that."

That's a relief. But what am I thinking? Only a few hours ago, I wanted to get rid of it. Now here I am hoping it's a genuine van Gogh. Still, genuine or not, I'm pretty sure people are trying to get their hands on it. Do I really want to keep on carrying it around inside my shirt?

Professor Bauer says, "Okay, Charlie. Enough with the showing off. How old do you think it is?"

Charlie shrugs. "Hard to say. But from the layers of grime built up on it, I'd say it could be thirty or forty years old, at least. I'm not all that familiar with van Gogh's work. Never seen one up close, of course. But whatever this painting is, you have to admit it's nice brush work. If it's a student copy, they must have done it over and over again to get it just right. You sure it can't be an original, James?"

"Fraid not, Charlie. It's pretty well documented that it was destroyed in a museum in Magdeburg, Germany. The town was not only bombed, there was also a fire storm. Burned down most of the town, not only the museum."

Should I tell them I have information that it was removed from the museum before it burned? No, better wait and see what they come up with on their own.

Charlie takes the painting out from under the scope and looks at it closely. "Well, James, whatever it is, it's kind of . . . good, you know?"

Professor Bauer laughs. "I think we would all agree that Vincent van Gogh had a pretty good eye for portraying nature, even if it is only a copy. That's all you can tell us? That it's old?"

Charlie shrugs again. "Well, if you want to pay for a chemical analysis, we could probably get a better idea of it's exact age."

Professor Bauer reaches out to take back the painting. "No need for that. It doesn't really matter. Thanks for you help, anyhow."

But Charlie doesn't seem to want to give the painting up. He picks up a pair of very strong-looking glasses from his workbench and closely examines my painting. Is he getting the same feeling I did when I first saw it, that it somehow draws you in? Maybe he already wants it for himself.

Charlie says, "Tell you what, James. I know a guy that owes me a favor. How about I take it to him and get him to do a chemical analysis? Okay?"

Professor Bauer again reaches for the painting. "I don't think so, Charlie. Scott here wants to believe it's the genuine article. He's been carrying it around inside his shirt. I don't think he'd be willing to let it out of his sight."

I step forward. "No, it's fine. Keep it. I mean, keep it long enough to get your friend to analyze it. I'd really like to know when it was made."

Charlie smiles, and turns to place it on his workbench.

Seeing it lying there on his workbench, at first, I sort of want to grab it and put it back inside my shirt. But no, it's better to find out once and for all what it really is.

But Professor Bauer doesn't seem all that happy about the idea of Charlie taking it. He's staring in the direction of the painting and frowning. Is he also getting caught up in the idea that he might be able to get it for himself? Finally, he says, "Okay, fine, Charlie. You have it checked out, but call me as soon as you find out anything, and I'll come get it."

"Sure," says Charlie. "I'll give my friend a call right now."

Professor Bauer and Charlie shake hands again, and this time Charlie also reaches out to shake my hand. He says, "Nice to meet you, son. Thanks for bringing it to me. It's . . . interesting."

Professor Bauer leads me out the door, and we head back toward the art building.

I stop. "You know, professor, now that somebody else is taking care of the painting, I'd better get back to doing what I'm supposed to be doing, being a student. I'd better go home and try to get caught up with my studies."

"Good idea, Scott. Focus on your studying and don't worry about the painting. Come back tomorrow at about this same time, and we'll go see what Charlie found out."

With a wave goodbye, he heads for the Art Building, and I head for my car.

As I walk, I notice, for the first time today, how nice and warm it is. It's amazing how distracted I've been. But I realize I'm feeling a little . . . I don't know, sort of . . . naked without the familiar feel of the little painting inside my shirt.

Twenty-Three

Back at my apartment, I've hardly gotten started reading one of my textbooks when the phone rings. I jump up and run to answer it. Is it Jill?

I pick up the phone, and I hardly get the word "Hello" out of my mouth when a husky male voice says, "If you ever want to see Jill again, you'll bring back the painting." Then, the line goes dead.

I'm left standing there with the silent phone in my shaking hand. Maybe I should have realized something like this was going to happen as soon as Jill disappeared. Why, oh why, didn't I just take the painting directly to Eichner as soon as I found it?

I hang the phone up and pace the room, trying to think what to do. Should I go back to the museum and get the painting? Maybe Charlie hasn't taken it to his friend yet.

But even if I get it back, what then? The threatening voice said I should "bring back" the painting. What does that mean? Bring it back where? To Eichner's old house? That doesn't make sense; they're going to tear that house down. And I can't take it to Eichner because he's no longer at the hospital.

But maybe Eichner is back. If so, I should go to Cottage H and tell him I don't have it anymore. I'll tell him it's at the university art museum. He can go there and try to convince them he's the rightful owner. The important thing is, if they know I no longer have the painting, they'll have to let Jill go.

I hurry out to my car and head for the hospital. As I drive, I can't stop my mind from imaging what kind of situation Jill is in. Is she tied to a chair somewhere, bound and gagged and scared out of her mind? I never should have let her get involved in this. I should have never got involved in this either. From the moment we found the painting, things have been getting weird. And dangerous. A man dressed in black chasing us. A dead body found in Eichner's old house. When will all this end? And how will it end.

Will I survive it, or will they find me dead in that old house also?

At the hospital, I park in my usual place and run as fast as I can into the administration building. I run right past the guard lady, but she calls me back, "Wait a minute, son. What's the hurry?"

"No time to talk right now, ma'am. "I've got to get to Cottage H."

"But I have some information for you."

Information? Does she know something about who has Jill? I hurry back to her. "Information for me? What kind of information?"

"About Fat Freddy.

"Fred? Do you know where he is?"

"Well, I found out for you, didn't I? Nobody talks to me. It's like they think I'm a statue or something. They go right past me like I'm not even here. So I asked them. I went to the Puerto Rican doctor and asked him. He's in the room next to Fred's. He said not to worry. He put Fred in the clinic. So there. See? I did it for you, didn't I? Now you know where he is."

"Fred is in the clinic? What's the clinic?"

"Oh, you don't know about the clinic? It's for treatable illnesses and such. The flu, or injuries. Things our foreign doctors can treat here, even though they're not real doctors yet. But if a patient gets real sick, we send them out to a regular hospital."

"Oh, okay. Thank you. Can you tell me how to find the clinic?"

"It's at the other end of the grounds. Follow the sidewalk all the way up there. You'll see it. It says clinic on the door."

I thank the woman again and hurry in the direction she pointed me. So Fred's disappearance doesn't actually have anything to do with the painting. Thank goodness for that, at least. He's just sick or something. But actually, I sure hope it's nothing serious.

I find the clinic, and as I wander the halls, I run into a very short, very thin foreign-looking man in a white coat. I say, "Can you help me? I'm looking for Fred. You know, Fat Freddy."

The little man says, "Yes, he here. But do not call him Fat. It disrespectful."

"Oh, no, I don't call him that. I just wanted you to know who I was looking for I mean . . . Oh, never mind. Is he here?"

"*Si.* I put him here. He live in room right next to me. Lucky it so. *Suerte,* you know?"

"So, he is here? What's the matter with him?"

"He bad sick. Diabetic attack. Ketoacidosis. Dangerous. He need insulin."

"Really? I didn't know he was diabetic."

"He not know too. But sure to come eventually. He eat too much. "

"Yeah, he sure does. I suppose you've got him on a diet. He'll hate that."

The doctor laughs. "He sure do hate diet. Says we kill him. But he getting better now."

"He's okay now? So I can see him?"

"Sure. Come. I show."

So this is the Puerto Rican doctor Fred mentioned. I guess Fred really was lucky to have a doctor living in the room next to his.

The doctor leads me down the hallway to a bright sunny room. Fred is there, propped up with pillows, watching TV.

The doctor turns down the TV and excuses himself.

I go to Fred's bedside. "So, here you are. I've been worried about you. I thought . . . well, never mind what I thought. I'm just glad you're okay."

Fred looks surprised. "They didn't tell you?"

"Who didn't tell me?"

"The Grimms. I sent word over to Cottage H that I was here so you wouldn't worry."

"No, they didn't tell me. But actually, I haven't been there much. I've been chasing down . . . uh, call it leads. About the painting."

"Great," says Fred, immediately cheering up. "You're just what the doctor ordered, if you know what I mean. Tell me all about it. But first, I hope you smuggled in some candy bars for me."

"No candy bars, Fred. But I do have some interesting news about the painting. Eichner ran off, and he told me he stole the painting from a museum in Germany. During the war."

Fred is all smiles. "Ah ha! Just what I said, right? I knew it was the genuine article as soon as I saw it."

"Well, we'll soon find out. I took it to the university art museum. They're going to do a technical analysis of it."

"Now that's the kind of good news I've been waiting for. I bet they'll find out it's a genuine van Gogh, and we'll be rich. Uh, . . . I mean, you'll be rich."

I decide against telling him about the police stopping me, or about Jill being kidnapped. No use worrying him while he's sick. I hate seeing good old Fred in a hospital bed. Seeing him like this reminds me of the many times I went to see my father in that terrible long-term care place they kept my father in while he was waiting to die. One large room with about twenty other old men, all of them just waiting to die. It was unbelievably depressing. My own father, along with all those other men, lined up in narrow little beds as if they were on a conveyer belt, ready to be pushed out the door right into their graves.

But here in this clinic, at least there's actually a visitor's chair. In that place my father was placed in, they didn't have any visitor chairs. On my first visit there, when I asked for a chair so I could sit next to my father's bed, it took them quite a while to go find one. That told me nobody else ever came to see any of the dying men. Or if they did, they didn't stay long enough to sit down. At the time, that confused me. Weren't these men somebody's father, somebody's husband? But then, my own mother only went with me to see him once, and then she swore she would never set foot in that terrible place again.. And she never did. It's like she just wrote him off. Even at his funeral, she wouldn't go look inside the casket. I understood why. Lying there in his casket, with all that ridiculous makeup they put on his face to make him look "better", he didn't look like the same person I'd known all my life. He was like a tiny, shrunken version of that big strong man.

"Hey, Earth to Scotty. Where did you go? Did I say something wrong?"

I realize I've been staring out the window. Am I wishing I was out there instead of here in this hospital room? "Oh, sorry, Fred. No, you didn't say anything wrong. I was just thinking."

"Oh yeah? Thinking about what?"

"Oh, just old memories. Nothing to do with you." I need to shake those old thoughts off. No reason for me to get all depressed about that again. Fred's room is nothing like the dreary room they stuck my father in. This room is pretty nice, with a sun-filled window right next to Fred's bed.

"Old memories, eh. Well, whatever they are, they must be some bad old memories. You got sad there all of a sudden, right in the middle of telling me good news. What is it you're not telling me?"

"Never mind, Fred. It's just that I don't like hospitals much. My father died when I was pretty young, and he spent a lot of time in hospitals before he died. I . . . well, I took it hard."

"I guess you're still dealing with it."

I wave off that idea. "It's all right. It just took me a long time to get over it."

"So your response to him dying made you retreat into yourself. I get it. I've seen the same thing in some of my kids, especially after they come back from their home visits. They come to class and just sit in the back row, all quiet. Refuse to talk, or even look at anybody. But I pull 'em out of it. I'm good at that. I give 'em candy and get 'em involved in the fun stuff we do in class. Sooner or later, I can snap 'em out of it."

Looking at Fred, I can see how he could help them. He may be an adult, but actually he's not all that much older than his students. He's grossly overweight, but he's always cheerful. And whenever we talk, he always wants to talk more about me than about himself. I bet he's the same way with his students.

He laughs. "There, you did it again. Went right back inside

yourself. Always thinking, aren't you? Okay, let's talk about it. What's on your mind?"

"Oh, it's just that damn painting. I wish I'd never got involved with it."

"Why? Has something bad happened?"

Should I tell him about what's happened to Jill? Fred seems pretty happy, but he is in a hospital bed recovering from a serious illness. When my father was in that dying place, I never talked to him about serious stuff. I always tried to cheer him up, even though sometimes he got mad at me for what he called "pandering" him.

Fred points at me. "There's that look again. Went inside again, didn't you? Come on, Scotty, you can tell me. What's wrong?"

"I didn't want to tell you, Fred, you being sick and all."

"Aw hell, I'm not sick anymore. They're gonna let me out of this place as soon as my vitals stabilize. So, what is it?"

"It's Jill, I'm really worried about her. They kidnapped her."

Fred looks completely startled. "Kidnapped? What're you talking about?"

I've never seen Fred look or act scared, but now the look on his face says he's probably as close as he ever gets to actually being scared. "Yeah, kidnapped. And it's about the painting. I got a phone call this morning saying if I ever wanted to see her again, I have to bring back the painting."

"Bring back? Bring back where?"

"I've been trying to figure that out myself. I can only think maybe the voice meant I should take the painting back to Eichner. But it wasn't Eichner's voice, and like I said, Eichner ran off."

"Maybe Eichner's not working alone. Maybe he's got henchmen."

"Yeah, I was thinking that too. Remember, I saw those two men in suits visiting him when he was in the ward dorm."

"Jesus, Scotty. This is getting damn serious. Maybe you should call the cops."

"I will, but first I'd better go over to Cottage H. If Eichner is back there, maybe he'll know what's going on. He might even know where Jill is. I'll tell him where to find the painting. Maybe they'll release Jill, and that'll be the end of it."

Fred nods thoughtfully. "Okay. Why don't you do that. Then come back and tell me what you find out. We'll figure this out together."

Twenty-Four

I tell Fred to hang in there and to get better soon. Then, I hurry to Cottage H, and as soon as I walk in the door, I know something's wrong because the Scribbler is trying to keep me from going in. I try to squeeze past him, but he keeps on moving his chair in front of me. And then the Growler appears and stands right in front of me with his muscular arms crossed in front of himself. The look on his face is as threatening as I've ever seen him, and of course, he's growling at me.

Skinny old Scribbler's not a problem, but the Growler is something else. I'm not sure I want to try to force my way past him.

I see Mrs. Grimm is at her usual place, looking over papers at her desk. I yell at her, "Mrs. Grimm, tell these idiots to let me in!"

My voice seems dramatically loud in this quiet ward, and it does get her attention.

The Growler turns to look at her, and she does some kind of quick gesture with her hand that he apparently takes to mean he should bring me to her.

I allow the Growler to get his iron grip on my arm and lead me, forcefully, to her.

She's not smiling as she says, "What seems to be the problem, Scott?"

I point at the Growler who is still standing close behind me, and still growling, of course. I try to make my voice sure and strong as I say, "No problem, just that they wouldn't let me into the ward."

She's got a grim look on her face, which is unusual for her, as she says, "Well, there's been some trouble on the ward. They're just being . . . careful."

I lean forward with both hands on her desk and look her right in her eyes. This time, I'm not going to let her put me off.

"Trouble? What kind of trouble?"

She does her typical wave of her hand to ward off my question. "Oh, nothing that should concern you, Scott."

"Well things *are* going on here on this ward that do concern me, Mrs. Grimm. When I was last here, your husband called me in to his office to ask me if I knew where Mr. Eichner had gone. Is that the trouble you're referring to?"

"Oh, you don't need to worry about that anymore. He has returned. We're keeping him in the dorm until he feels better."

"Better? Is something wrong with him?"

She again does her little wave. "No, he just needs rest."

I'm getting tired of her always putting me off. She's treating me like a kid or something. I point toward the dorm and say, "I'd better go back to the dorm and talk to him. He . . . uh, likes to talk to me." I turn to head in that direction, but the Growler blocks my way. I try to step around him, but he moves in front of me, so close that I can smell his sweat. I once again realize that the Growler is so big that despite his age, he could actually hurt me, maybe really bad.

I turn back to Mrs. Grimm. "Why is the Growler acting so . . . aggressive toward me? We've always gotten along all right before."

Mrs. Grimm doesn't answer my question, she just holds her hand out toward the Growler and does a funny kind of flick with her fingers. Whatever that finger flick meant, it does get the Growler to back off.

As I push my way past him, Mrs. Grimm calls after me, "You can do your usual walking and observing, Scott, but don't go into the dorm. Mr. Eichner needs his rest."

I walk away from her, intentionally not heading in the direction of the dorm. But after a few trips through the ward, just observing that there is nothing new to observe, I decide to swing by the dorm. I should at least peek in there to make sure Eichner is all right. And if I get a chance, I'll duck in there and ask him what he found out at the demolition site.

As I walk, it's clear that both the Scribbler, who is back taking imaginary notes at his station by the door, and the Growler, who is back at his station against the wall, growling, are both keeping their eyes on me. If I'm going to duck into the dorm to talk to Eichner, I'll have to be quick about it.

Finally, on about my fifth trip through the ward, they both seem to have relaxed a bit. And Mrs. Grimm has gone back to her paperwork. This is my chance. I nonchalantly pass close to the dorm, and then I duck inside.

As soon as my eyes adjust to the dim light in the dorm, I spot Eichner in his usual bed. But he's not alone. The two men in dark suits, the men Eichner told me were Israelis, are there with him, leaning over him and talking to him in loud voices. He seems to be arguing with them and trying to push them away.

I immediately run toward them, although I don't have any idea of what's going on. I yell, "Hey, leave him alone."

One of the men immediately jerks Eichner up out of his bed. The other man comes toward me.

I try to get past him, but he's bigger and stronger than I am. He holds me off as I see the other man hustle Eichner farther back into the dorm. He's forcing Eichner to walk by holding one of Eichner's arms pinned behind his back.

Eichner shouts, "Help me, Scott."

The man quickly clamps his hand over Eichner's mouth.

I yell, "Stop that! Leave him alone." I try to go help him, but the man who's confronting me pushes me back.

I look past him and see where the other man is taking Eichner: there's a door at the very back corner of the dorm. Is it a fire-escape door? Is he going to take Eichner out through that door?

I try to force my way past the big guy that's holding me back, but he gets ahold of the front of my jacket and uses some kind of leg kick to the back of my ankle that takes me right down to the floor onto my back. Thankfully, he keeps a hold on my jacket to make sure I don't bang my head on the floor. He holds me down and says, "Be quiet. Do not move." He has a heavy foreign accent.

I start to protest more, but he suddenly turns away from me and runs to join his partner.

As I scramble to my feet, I see that both men have ahold of Eichner by the arms, and they're rushing him out through that door.

I run to the door, but it's locked.

I run out of the dorm, straight to Mrs. Grimm. I point back toward the dorm. "They've kidnapped him!"

She doesn't seem all that surprised as she says, "Kidnapped? What in heaven's name are you talking about?"

I'm out of breath, but I manage to get out, "Eichner. Two men. They took him."

"Did you go into the dorm? Didn't I tell you not to do that?"

"I only looked in. As I was passing. I saw two men. They took him out a door back there." I point again.

She nods. "I think you should talk to Mr. Grimm." She turns to look at her husband's door.

Mr. Grimm is exactly the person I do want to talk to. I hurry past her desk and go knock on the door to his apartment. Without even waiting for a response, I knock again, louder.

Soon, he opens the door, but this time I don't go into his lair. Instead, I remain outside his door, and I try to remain calm as I tell him about the two men who took Eichner.

He smiles and nods, as if he's being patient with me.

I'm beginning to hate that condescending smile. I say, "Well, aren't you going to do anything about it?"

He says, "I think you should come in and sit down, Scott. You need to calm down."

"No, I don't want to come in, and I don't need to calm down! Some weird shit is going on here. I tell you two men have just kidnapped one of your patients, and it's like you don't even care."

"No, Scott, they haven't kidnapped Mr. Eichner. Those two men are members of a police force, and they had a legitimate warrant for his arrest."

"Are they Israelis?"

"That's right."

"What right do Israelis have to come in here and arrest a patient?"

"As I said, they had a legal warrant."

"And you just let them walk in and take him? And how did they get a key to that back door in the dorm. Did you give it to them?"

The condescending smile quickly disappears from Mr. Grimm's face. "Now why would you say that, Scott? Has Mr. Eichner been telling you his high tales again?"

"He said you were getting paid by the Israelis. Are you?"

"Listen, Scott. I told you the Israelis have a legal warrant for his arrest. They said he was a guard in a German concentration camp during the war."

"No, he was a guard in a gallery. An art gallery."

Mr. Grimm gets a sad look on his face and shakes his head. "Sorry, son. I'm afraid you've been taken in by Eichner's tall tales. I can assure you the Israelis have a solid case against him for war crimes. They have proof. Now, why don't you just go back to doing what you're supposed to be doing. Observing and learning." He leads me out of his apartment.

Now it's my turn to shake my head. "No, what I should be doing is reporting what's going on here at Cottage H. I'm sure the authorities at this hospital would like to know more about what's going on here. Not only did you let them take Eichner away, but I think they'd like to know more about how you're treating the patients here. You're treating them like trained rats."

"Trained rats? I can't imagine what you're thinking, son. Maybe you're having some kind of breakdown. I think you need to sit down and rest for a while." He turns and gives some kind of hand signal to his wife, who I now see has been watching us. She in turn, gives the same kind of hand signal to the Growler who immediately comes toward me.

I say, "Oh, no you don't, Mr. Grimm. You can't use your enforcer to treat me like one of your trained patients."

The Growler keeps coming, and he grabs ahold of the back of my neck. I can feel his grip tightening on my neck, and I've never felt anything like the pain it elicits. He's forcing me to walk, and although I try to resist, the pain in the back of my neck is so intense there's nothing I can do but go wherever he wants me to go.

Turns out, he wants me to go to one of the chairs that are lined up in front of the TV. Does he now think I'm one of the patients?

He forces me to sit down, but as soon as he lets go of my neck and walks away, I jump up and head for the front door. I've got to get off of this ward, and quick.

But the Growler is right back, and he's got ahold of the back of my neck again. His grip is incredibly strong, so strong he's able to force me right back down into the same chair. Then, he leans down and puts his face right in front of mine. This time, he not only growls, he also bares his jagged teeth at me.

I get it. Despite his lack of language, I know he's telling me to stay put or else he'll hurt me more.

I look at the old men sitting around me. None of them will look at me. Most of them seem to be just staring straight ahead, seeing nothing. A few of them might actually be paying a bit of attention to the TV which seems to be showing some kind of inane game show in which people are trying to guess the price of groceries. Are these old men willing to just sit here all day look-ing at that kind of nonsense? You'd think they'd refuse, but maybe in the past somebody tried to resist and they got hurt. Maybe every one of these old men has felt the Growler's painful vice-like grip on the back of their heads, so they've all learned to just sit quietly. Is that what it takes to survive on this ward? Is it what I also have to do to survive? That's a scary thought. How did I get myself into this? Apparently, my threat to report Mr. Grimm to the authorities worried him a lot more than I thought it would. Does he plan to keep me here forever to stop me from doing that? Maybe I should go tell him I changed my mind, that I won't report him.

But he won't want to take that chance. I'd better just get the heck out of here.

I turn to look back at the front door. The Scribbler has placed his chair right in front of it. He's old and weak looking. I could probably just knock him out of the way. Or, maybe I can convince these old men to help me. I could tell them that we can all get off this ward if we get together and rush him at once.

But what about the Growler? He looks damn strong. Is one of his jobs to make sure the patients don't try to get off this ward? In my first interview with Mr. Grimm, he said Cottage H is an open ward, but if any of the patients talked to me about wanting to get off the ward, I should tell them to go talk to him. So far, I haven't seen one of them try to get out that door.

The Growler is back at his station against the wall, and he's keeping his eyes on me. He's big, but he's also old. Maybe I could make it to the front door faster than he could respond.

As if he's reading my mind, he comes toward me. I quickly turn away from him and pretend to be watching the TV.

The Growler is standing right next to me with his big arms crossed in front of himself. Did Mr. Grimm tell him to keep a close eye on me? If I try to make a run for the door, he'll grab me before I can even get going. I guess I'm stuck right here in this chair if I don't want to get my neck broken.

But how long do they think they can keep me here? Don't they know that sooner of later, someone will miss me and come looking for me?

But who actually knows I'm here? Nobody except Fred, and he's ill, stuck in the clinic. Even if Fred gets out of the clinic and starts to wonder why I don't ever come to see him, he might think I'm at the university or too busy studying. Fred doesn't even know where I live. I might be stuck here for a long time. Forever? I'm having troublesome visions of growing old on this ward, seeing myself lined up every morning to be drugged into submission.

No, I have to be more logical about this. They can't keep me here forever. Maybe I can sneak out in the night. That's what Eichner did.

But what if they keep a close watch on me day and night?

I try to stay calm and think this through. I can't let fear run away with me. But the idea of maybe being locked up on this ward forever has got me sweating, and I can feel my leg starting to shake. I can't seem to stop it. Why am I getting so scared? What can they do to me besides keep me in this chair? Kill me? Could they get away with that? Maybe.

I look up at the Growler, and of course, he growls at me. Maybe I should try to fight him. It might be my only chance to escape before . . . before they what? Kill me? Wait, they don't need to kill me, they'll just drug me until I'm like all these old men, sitting stupidly in front of this stupid TV.

I hear a commotion, and the Growler hurries way. I turn and see that the Scribbler seems to be trying to block someone from coming onto the ward. The Growler is hurrying to try to help the Scribbler, and Mrs. Grimm is also hurrying in that direction.

I take their distraction as an opportunity to jump up and run toward the door. Maybe I can slip past them in the commotion.

As I get closer, I see who it is. It's Fred! Good old Fred. He's come to save me. I yell, "I'm here, Fred! Thank goodness you're here."

Fred waves at me, and says, "What's going on here, Scotty?"

The Scribbler is dancing around in front of Fred, futilely trying to push him back out the door.

Fred throws him out of his way as if he's nothing more than a bothersome gnat.

The Growler tries to push Fred back out the door, but Fred uses both hands to push him backwards, and he does it with such force that the Growler stumbles backward and falls down onto his butt. Surprisingly, he doesn't even try to get back up.

Before I can get there, Mrs. Grimm has arrived, and she's confronting Fred. She says, "Excuse me, sir, whoever you are, you have no right to come into this ward."

Fred puts his face in hers and yells, "Hell with that, lady. I'm the hospital schoolteacher at this institution, and I can go onto any ward anytime I want to. And why would you want to stop me anyhow? I've heard about some weird shit going on in this ward. I think it may be time for my friends in hospital administration to investigate this place."

Mrs. Grimm turns and hurries away, probably to go get Mr. Grimm. The Growler trails after her, leaning forward with his head down like a chastised schoolboy.

As soon as I get to Fred, he claps me on the back and says, "What's wrong, Scotty? You look like you're scared shitless."

I grab his hand as if I'm going to shake it, but I keep hold of his hand and try to drag him off the ward. "Let's get out of here fast, Fred. I'll tell you all about it."

Fred looks back once, and then follows me out the door.

Twenty-Five

As soon as we're out of Cottage H, I hurry Fred along the sidewalk, trying to get as far from Cottage H as possible and as quick as possible. But I'm not sure where we should go. "Wait a minute, Fred. Aren't you supposed to be in the clinic?"

"Naw. I checked myself out of that place. Had to get back to my schoolroom. Who knows what my kids have been up to without me?"

"So, we're . . . uh, heading for your classroom?"

"Right."

"Good. They were trying to keep me in Cottage H. That big guy you had to push out of your way. They call him the Growler. He's their enforcer. He got ahold of the back of my neck and about broke it. I was scared he really might do it."

Fred is staring at me. "Growler? Enforcer? What are you talking about? Any why would they want to keep you there?"

"It's complicated, Fred. When we get to your classroom, I'll tell you all about it."

Fred grins. "Okay, but you'll be happy to see who's waiting for you there."

"Someone is waiting for me?"

"Yep. Jill."

I stop walking. "Jill is here? Right now? They let her go?"

"I guess so. I didn't take time to talk to her. I just parked her in my classroom and came to Cottage H to find you." He grabs my arm to get me walking again. "Come on. Let's get there quick. I've got some great candy bars stashed there in a secret place where the kids can't find 'em. We can have a picnic."

We reach Fred's schoolroom, but there are no students there. Fred whispers, "I'm gonna go get my secret stash of candy bars." As he heads for a closet, he points toward the front of the room, and I see Jill. She's sitting in one of the student chairs, facing the front blackboard. Boy, am I glad to see her. She turns and sees me, and then jumps up and runs to me.

I give her a big hug, and say, "Boy am I glad to see you. I got a phone call that said they were holding you until they got the painting back."

"What?" she says. "Holding me?"

"That's what they said."

"Well, no one was actually holding me. Not exactly. I was at the city hospital after my granddad had a heart attack, and a doctor—at least I thought he was a doctor—came in and said I had to stay put in my granddad's hospital room until further notice because there was an outbreak of some kind of contagious illness on the ward. He said they had to isolate everybody for a while. But eventually, when I saw people walking by, I went out and asked a nurse if the isolation was over. She didn't have any idea of what isolation I was talking about. I went back to grand-dad's room while I tried to figure it out."

"Your granddad is in the hospital? What happened to him?"

She reaches out to take my hand. "Oh, Scott. My granddad had a heart attack. The ambulance drivers were nice and let me ride along with him to the hospital. I've been there with him ever since. They let me sleep in a cot in his room."

I keep hold of her hand as I say, "Oh, no. How is he?"

"They operated on his heart, and now they say he's recovering well. Anyhow, when I found out I didn't have to remain in isolation, I started wondering if maybe you might be looking for me." She blushes, and then quickly says, "To tell me about the painting, I mean. But you never told me where you lived, and I didn't have your phone number. So I came here because you told me you were doing training or something at a mental hospital. The cab driver said there was only one mental hospital in town, so he brought me here. I asked the lady guard at the front entrance if she knew you. She said you were up at the clinic visiting your friend Fred. I ran into Fred just as he was coming out of the clinic's front door. He was friendly. Asked me who I was, and when I told him, he brought me here to his classroom. He said I should wait here while he went to find you."

I give her another hug, longer this time, and then I suggest we sit down so I can tell her about everything that's happened. We sit in two of the student chairs, and I say, "I'm sure glad you came, Jill. You won't believe what's happened since I saw you last. I kept going by your house, but you were never there."

Fred returns with a big handful of candy bars. He sits down and hands one to Jill and another one to me. He tears into the first of his bars and gulps it down in two bites before opening another one. Speaking with his mouth full, he says, "Hungry. Held off eating until I went to find you."

"I'll take that as a big compliment, Fred, but let me tell you both what's been going on. It's a complicated story. I'll start with the most recent thing. The Israelis took Eichner away."

Fred is about to take another big bite of his candy car, but pauses, staring at me. "The Israelis took Eichner? What Israelis?"

"Those two men I told you about. The men that were talking to Eichner in the dorm. Turns out they were Israelis, and they said Eichner committed war crimes. As a guard in a German concentration camp. But that doesn't make sense. Eichner told me he was a guard in the local art gallery, not in any kind of prison camp."

Jill says, "Do you believe him?"

"Well, he might have a tendency to make up stories, but how else could he have gotten his hands on the painting?"

Jill says, You're losing me. Are you saying the painting is for sure real? That he stole it from an art museum?"

"Well, it's either a real van Gogh or a very good student copy done a long time ago. That's what they told me at the university."

Fred pauses his eating long enough to say, "I think it's the genuine article. Why else would so many people be trying to get their hands on it?"

"Well, maybe, or maybe not. Anyhow, back to the situation at Cottage H. After I threatened to report what the Grimms were doing there, they wouldn't let me off the ward. Fred came just in time to rescue me."

"I'll take care of that," says Fred. The head nurse is a friend of mine. She'll get an investigation of that ward going, and quick."

Jill stands up. "Well, you've certainly got my head spinning, Scott. But I've got to get back to the hospital to be with my granddad."

"Let me drive you," I say. "I'll tell you more on the way."

She gives my hand a little squeeze and says, "I'd like that." Keeping ahold of my hand, she smiles at Fred. "Nice to meet you, Fred. And thank you for the candy bar."

Fred says, "Any friend of Scott's is a friend of mine. Actually, after everything Scott told me about you, I've been wanting to meet you."

Jill seems surprised by his words and turns to look at me.

"He's kidding," I quickly say. "Fred is quite the kidder."

"I am a kidder," says Fred, "but I can be serious too, and I think you'd both better be careful out there. Don't forget somebody is still looking for that painting, and it appears that they want it bad."

"Don't worry, Fred. Now that the Israelis took Eichner away, I have the feeling that this will all soon be over. And as soon as I drop Jill off, I'll swing by the university art museum to see what they found out about the painting."

Fred says, "Okay. And then come back and tell me what you find out. I'm going to my room to rest. As soon as I get caught up on some paperwork here.

I say, "Will do."

Jill and I go out the door, still holding hands. As we walk to my car, I think about Fred's words urging caution. He's probably right. With Eichner gone, that kills my plan to give the painting back to him. I'm again wondering if I should just give it to the university art museum. On the other hand, Jill said she was trying to save money to go to the university. If I can sell the painting, we could end up going to the university together.

Jill says, "What are you thinking about?"

I shrug and say, "I guess I'm just thinking about all the crazy stuff that's happened since we found that little painting."

She does a funny little smile and says, "Yeah, I've been thinking a lot about the painting too. While I was sitting with my granddad there in the hospital, I kept on remembering how we went into that old house and found it." She again squeezes my hand.

I'm liking the feeling of her holding my hand as we walk. In fact, I'm liking it very much. I say, "Yeah. And the best part about it, I think, was meeting you."

She smiles again and keeps ahold of my hand all the way to my car.

Twenty-Six

After I drop Jill off at the hospital, I drive straight to the university. I'm not sure if Charlie will talk to me at the art museum unless Professor Bauer is with me, so I hurry to the professor's office. I sure hope he'll be there.

I'm in luck. The professor's office door is open, and I can see that he's reading a book. It's a large book, probably a book about paintings. Is he studying van Gogh?

I tap on the door frame to get his attention.

He looks up at me and smiles. "Ah, there you are. I wondered when you were going to show up."

"Uh, I've been . . . busy."

"Charlie called. He said your painting has come back from the technical experts, and he has some interesting information. Want to walk over there?"

"You bet. I'm eager to find out what they said."

As we walk, the closer we get to the museum, the more excited I'm getting. With what Eichner told me, I now know it could actually be the real van Gogh painting that he rescued from that museum in Germany. I hope the experts will agree.

The professor talks about the nice weather, and he points out all the new construction on campus. He says, "You know, the new crop of students every fall always seems younger than the year before." He chuckles at this own joke, and I smile to show him I get it.

Interesting that he doesn't seem to want to talk about the painting. In fact, he continues talking about everything and anything but the painting. It makes me wonder if it's his way of toning down my expectations.

But it's actually having the opposite effect on me. His attitude is making me wonder if he's taking me to the museum to spring a happy surprise on me. Maybe he already knows the painting is a genuine van Gogh.

The professor knocks on the museum's back door, and Charlie quickly opens it. He's all smiles as he welcomes us into his workshop.

I see the little painting lying on his workbench, and I'm grateful to see that the technicians haven't damaged it. At least it doesn't look damaged from where I'm standing.

Charlie shakes Professor Bauer's hand and says, "Apparently, we got lucky. They've got something of a van Gogh expert over there. She said . . . well, I'll just tell you what I got from her report. He picks up a piece of typewritten paper from his workbench and says, "You'll be interested to learn that the painting is old."

Charlie is talking to Professor Bauer as if I'm not there, but I can't stand it anymore, so I jump in with, "How old?"

He turns to look at me. "Her report only says it's not a recent copy. If it is a copy, it's a pretty old one. She says the canvas is old and the oil paints are old, but it's in pretty good shape. It needs to be cleaned, but it's obviously been kept away from sunlight and environmental contaminants. Maybe in a museum."

But I know it hasn't been in a museum. It's been hidden up there in Eichner's attic. Turns out, it's lucky that Eichner kept it hidden away for so many years in a tightly sealed box under his attic floor.

Charlie looks up from the report. "She says to know more, you'd have to have the paints chemically analyzed."

Professor Bauer says, "Does she say how much that would cost?"

Charlie shakes his head. "No, but she does warn that it would be expensive. Probably not worth it, she says, because we have such good verified testimony that it was destroyed in the war. She did some research and got confirmed information that everything in the Kaiser-Friedrich Museum in Magdeburg, Germany, where it was housed, was destroyed in the war."

I can hardly keep myself from blurting out that I have information that someone stole this particular painting from that museum before it was destroyed, but I decide to keep quiet.

Charlie continues to read from the paper: she goes on quite a bit about what an analysis of the paint would tell us, saying that the reds and yellows do seem to be fading, like the oil paints of that era are prone to do. She says synchrotron X-ray diffraction would tell us if the paint is of the type van Gogh actually used. For example if it contains any cochineal red pigment, a red pigment made of organic compounds. The problem is, she says, more modern pigments were becoming commercially available in the late nineteenths century, and van Gogh is known to have used some of them. When he could afford it. So, it might not contain any of the old organic paint."

Professor Bauer says, "Okay, enough of her showing off. Doesn't she have an opinion? About what it really is, I mean."

Still looking at the paper, Charlie says, "Yeah, she speculates that it could be a copy made while it was still in that German museum. She says it's a very good copy, made by a somebody that must have studied van Gogh's impasto methods."

Again, I can't contain myself. I ask, "But does she think it's valuable?"

Charlie nods. "Yes, she does address that. She doesn't think it's valuable, because it's only a copy, but she says some collector might pay to get it so he could tell the story of how the original was destroyed, and only this copy remains."

Professor Bauer shakes Charlie's hand and says, "Well, all good information. Thanks for doing that. I owe you one."

"No problem," says Charlie. "Maybe the next time we go out to dinner, you could take me to a good restaurant instead of the cheap Chinese places you usually take me to."

Professor Bauer winks at him. "It's a deal. See you then."

Charlie hands me the painting, and I have to resist the urge to do my usual thing and hide it under my shirt.

As we're walking back toward the art building, Professor Bauer says, "I think you should keep it. Get a nice frame and put it on your wall. It wouldn't cost you much, and then you could do what that lady expert said, tell your friends the story of how the original was destroyed during the war."

I thank him and tell him I've got to go get some studying done.

He agrees and pats me on the back. "Right you are. You are a student, and a student's job is to study. By they way, if you want to learn more about art history, why not sign up for my class next semester. It's usually restricted to art majors, but I can get you in."

"Thank you, professor. After all this, I do think I'd like to learn more about art history."

As I head for my car, I hide the painting inside my shirt. Before I turn toward the parking lot, I glance back and see that Professor Bauer is still watching me. I wave goodbye to him, and I think he's chuckling to himself as he heads toward the art building.

Twenty-Seven

I drive straight to my apartment. After all the distractions, I've got to get some serious studying done or I'm going to flunk all my psych classes on my first semester as an actual psychology major.

But when I get to my apartment building, I stay in my car to think. Maybe I should go to Fred's room to tell him what I found out about the painting. And then I could also go see Jill and her granddad at the city hospital. On the other hand, they're not expecting to see me until tomorrow, and I really do need to get some studying done.

Before I get out, I watch the old foreign lady give the sidewalk yet another good sweeping. She's even sweeping the dirt between the sidewalk and the front of the apartment building. Obsessive-compulsive, I bet.

That thought reminds me that my clinical practices class is in the morning. What am I going to tell them about what I've been learning at the mental hospital? Obviously, I can't tell them everything. They'd be totally confused if I tried to explain about Eichner and the painting and the Israelis taking him away. But maybe I should at least tell them about how the Grimms have managed to control the old men on the ward, mostly with punishment. They'd be interested in that. Maybe I should tell them about how the Grimms tried to keep me prisoner on the ward. Professor Spence said they would be evaluating the on-site experience program next semester. Maybe I should tell somebody about the potential dangers there.

Finally, I get out of the car and head for my apartment. I really do need to get some studying done.

But before I can go into my apartment, the old sweeping lady stops me by putting her broom in my way. "A man. He look for you."

"A man? Looking for me?

"*Goy. Konflikt.*"

Goy. A Jewish word. So she's Jewish. And from her heavy accent, I doubt that she's been in this country very long. I say, "Uh, I know what *goy* means, but . . ?"

"*Konflikt.* Mean trouble. I say him go away. Painting all gone."

At first I'm not even sure I heard her right. Didn't she mention the painting? How could she know anything about that? And who was the man? It can't be one of the Israelis that kidnapped Eichner; she said he was a *Goy.* And why would this old woman tell the "*goy*" that the painting was now gone? It isn't gone. Is she trying to protect me ?

"Eichner gone too." She spits into the dirt. "Good riddance."

"Excuse me, ma'am, you said the name Eichner. How do you know him?"

"He come. He gone. They take away now. Good riddance." She spits into the dirt again.

She not only knows Eichner, she knows he's been taken away. And she has such strong negative feelings about him, she can't keep herself from spitting at the thought of him.

She turns away from me and goes back to her incessant sweeping.

I watch her sweep, trying to figure out how this old woman who I always see out here, day and night, doing her non-stop sweeping, could know anything about Eichner and the painting.

The only possible answer is that Eichner must have come here looking for me. And he must have asked her if I had a small painting. And then, somebody else came, a *Goy.* None of what she's saying makes sense.

I give up trying to figure it out, and decide I'd better get inside my apartment. Issues about the painting seem to keep on wanting to keep me from getting any studying done, but I'd better get to it if I'm going to pass my classes.

Twenty-Eight

Once I'm inside my apartment, I lock the door and do what has now become a ritual—I examine every inch of the place to determine if anybody has been inside.

Everything seems just as I left it. And if anybody had been inside my place, wouldn't the old Jewish sweeper lady have told me? Hopefully, they believed her, and now they think the painting is gone.

I take the painting out of my shirt and sit down on my couch/bed to look at it. As old and dirty looking at it is, it's still a really nice picture.

And then I remember what Professor Bauer told me about how to clean it. He said to use my own spit and some Q-Tips to make it look better. Do I dare do that? Would I ruin it?

Well, the experts said it was only a copy and wasn't all that valuable. And Professor Bauer as much as said the painting belongs to me now, so why not?

I leave the painting on the kitchen counter and go to the bathroom to get a handful of Q-Tips. I begin doing what the professor said, using my spit to clean it. I start in one corner, and it doesn't take me long to get about one square inch of the corner cleaned. I hold the painting up to the light. The little bit of cleaned corner does look better than the rest. The colors in that corner of the painting are noticeably brighter. More vibrant. It's really lucky that it was hidden away for so many years in Eichner's attic.

That little bit of corner I cleaned looks so good, I decide to keep at it.

It takes a long time, but eventually I manage to get the whole painting cleaned. I hold it up to the light, and to my eye, it looks great! I'm certainly no expert, but to me, it's quite a captivating picture. Maybe that's why van Gogh got so famous; he was able to give everyday people a fresh way to look at the beauty of nature. I sure don't know anything about art or artists, but I think I'd like to. Maybe I should do what Professor Bauer said and sign up for his art history class next semester.

But for now, I'm still a psychology student, and I've frittered away half the night cleaning the painting. I've got to get busy and start studying.

I find some tape and tape the painting to the wall, making sure that no sunlight will come though the window and shine on it in the morning.

Twenty-Nine

My alarm clock wakes me up at lot earlier than I'd like, but I force myself to get up and get moving. I didn't get much sleep, but I did get some studying done. Now I've got to get a move on if I'm going to get to the university in time for my clinical practices class.

I wish I had time to go to the hospital and tell Fred what I found out. I'll do that after my class. And then, I'll go to the hospital to see Jill and her granddad. She'll be happy to learn that I get to keep the painting.

At the university, before I even get to the parking lot, I can smell tear gas in the air. I guess something must have happened in Vietnam that set off yet another big on-campus demonstration, and that resulted in the police being called in again. Maybe President Nixon ordered another big offensive. Do I dare go to the central fountain to try to find out what's going on?

No, I could get swept up in the melee and accidentally end up getting arrested myself. The last time the police came on campus, they formed a perimeter and arrested everybody inside of it. The next day, the word on campus was that hundreds of innocent students got arrested and ended up lying face down all night in a fenced-in parking lot somewhere downtown. Of course, that set off another campus demonstration.

It means I should park off campus and get to my class without going through the center of the campus.

Luckily, I'm able to find a parking place over by the fraternity houses. It's a long walk to the psych building, but it gives me time to think about what I'm going to tell the class about my experiences at the mental hospital. But it's hard to focus because the strong smell of tear gas in the air keeps on reminding me about the war and the anti-war demonstrations. Until all this stuff about Eichner and the painting started happening, I was like everybody else, paying close attention to the televised news reports of what was going on in the war "over there." And every time, after watching the horror of it play out on TV, I'd end up trying to imagine myself getting drafted and ending up over there. I guess I've been using all the things going on with Eichner and the painting to avoid thinking about that. The last time I watched TV, they were saying the US is losing that war, and that it might be over soon. But would Nixon let that happen? Would he let our glorious military lose a war for the first time in US history? Not likely. And for that reason, I might yet get drafted and end up in Vietnam. But would I go? Lots of the other male students of my age are saying they won't go, even if they do get drafted. Some are even burning their draft cards. A lot of good that will do. Some are saying they will run away to Canada, or fake an injury. One guy said he thought he could get a doctor to say he has "heel spurs," something he claims is hard to verify.

I have no idea what I'll do if I get drafted. All I know is the whole war deal over there is Cold War nonsense, the U.S. and Russia vying to control different parts of the world. But I'd better not let myself get to thinking about all that. I should just concentrate on my studies. And now that I have two new friends, I should be grateful for that and spend as much time with them as possible.

Despite the long walk from off campus, I make it to my clinical practices class on time and sit in my usual chair. The other students straggle in, all of them talking about the big anti-war demonstration and the huge police presence on campus. A few of the usual students are missing. I wonder if they're participating in the demonstration. When they come back to class, will they look at me, wondering why I didn't participate also? If they say anything, what will I say? I don't want to insult them by telling what I really think, that their demonstrations won't do any good. In fact, Nixon and the other pro-war politicians will just use the "anti-American" student demonstrations to rile up the voters to get what they want, more war.

I'm still thinking about that when Professor Spence arrives. He doesn't mention the demonstrations or the smell of tear gas in the air, he just begins lecturing. The only reference to it is in his statement, "I hope you've all read at least some of the books I put on reserve at the library. That's assuming you could get there without being arrested."

He wasn't smiling as he said it, and in fact, I have the feeling that he's a bit disgusted about it all. But is he disgusted that the students are demonstrating instead of going to class, or is he disgusted that the university administration allowed the city police to come onto campus? Hard to say.

He says, "As you'll read in those reserved books at the library, the history of innovation in the treatment of mental illness is a troubled one. Because so many different treatment methods have been tried and failed over the years, many practicing psychologists and psychiatrists have become disentranced with any and all treatment methods and just rely on drugs to control inappropriate behavior. The discovery of anti-psychotics started with the first antihistamines all the way back in the 1940s. These drugs provided a chemical template from which a wide range of drugs useful in psychiatry were developed. They work like a key fitted into a lock, the receptor, but they do not turn the lock. Instead, they block access to what could be considered to be the natural key to the lock. In 1954, for the first time, a behavior-suppressing drug, chlorpromazine, brand name Thorazine, started being used as a treatment for mental disorders. Within ten years, more than fifty million prescriptions for Thorazine were known to have been filled. A lot of it was in use in mental hospitals."

His mention of drugs and mental hospitals makes me think of the morning lineup at Cottage H. I cautiously raise my hand.

The professor points at me. "You have a comment?"

"Uh, yes. Last time, you asked me to observe what treatment methods are being used at the local mental hospital."

He nods. "That's right. You were going to observe and report back to us. Were you going to make a comment about anti-psychotic drug use there?"

"Yes. I mean sort of. I don't know what kinds of drugs they're using, but on the ward I've been assigned to, first thing every morning, they line up, and they make the old men patients take pills. I don't know what kind of pills they're using. There are several different kinds, in big bottles."

The professor stares at me. "Are you suggesting it is the ward aides that determine what pills they patients get?"

"Uh, yes. I mean, I think so. The aide, Mr. Grimm, doesn't seem to be looking at any list on paper or anything. I guess he knows the patients so well, he knows what kind of pills they need."

"Is this ward aide you are describing, this *Mister* Grimm, a trained professional or . . . ?"

"No, he says he's not any kind of psychologist or anything. He and his wife, Mrs. Grimm, have been in charge of Cottage H for a long time, longer than I've been alive."

The professor continues to stare at me as if he isn't sure he can believe what I'm telling him. Is what I'm telling him so unusual? How would I know what's normal in a mental hospital? Cottage H is the only mental ward I've ever been on. "Anyhow, that's what I wanted to tell you about drugs." I look at the other students who are all paying rapt attention to what I'm saying. "I mean what I wanted to tell the class. The ward I've been assigned to isn't anything like what you see in the movies. You walk onto the ward, and its dead silence. Not a sound, and nobody is moving. It's true that it's an old men's ward, but they're not even talking to each other. They don't even get up and move around. They just sit, all day long. I mean . . . could the drugs be so powerful to make them act like that?"

The professor shakes his head. "Not normally. Unless they're overdosing them. Do you think that's what is happening?"

I shrug. "I wouldn't know how to tell about that. But I have seen them using punishment to stop just about any sort of behavior."

"Punishment?"

"Yeah. They use one of the patients, a really big guy known as the Growler. If a patient does something they don't like, making noise or something, they use him to stop it."

One of the other students, the same young guy with a budding beard that spoke up last time, says, "You've got to be kidding. The ward managers are using patients to punish other patients."

I say, "Yeah. I was shocked too, the first time I saw it."

He says, "Maybe it was just two patients getting into it. I bet that's not all that unusual."

I don't want to get into an argument with him, but the professor did ask me to report to the class what I've been seeing at the mental hospital, so I decide to answer him with the truth. "It was pretty clear to me that he was doing the bidding of the ward managers."

He says, "I doubt that."

The guy seems like he still doesn't believe what I'm saying. For some reason, I begin to wonder if he was one of the students participating in the anti-war demonstration earlier this morning. Maybe he's mad at me because he's never seen me at any of their demonstrations. I quietly say, "Mostly, that Growler guy just stands around growling at everybody. But they use him in the morning to make sure all the patients take their pills. And they use him to line everybody up. He put the pills in their mouths, and then pours water down their throats."

Professor Spence says, "Perhaps such things are not all that unusual. I was just reading about a new study done at another university that was designed to evaluate guard behavior in a simulated prison setting. They recruited students to play the guards and other students to play the role of prisoners. The researchers were shocked when the students playing the role of guards started mistreating the students playing the role of prisoners. The prisoner students, in response, escalated the confrontations."

The professor pauses, as if to gauge the students' reactions. They do seem shocked by what he's saying. Are they imagining how they would react if they were recruited for such an experiment? If I was in that experiment, would I start mistreating the students playing the role of the prisoners? I doubt it. But maybe the students who participated in the experiment also doubted they would act that way. But they did.

The professor, interestingly, looks at each of us in turn before he goes on. "The point being, if middle-class university students, playing the roles of guards and prisoners in a prison simulation, would act that way, how can we expect the poorly-paid guards in a real prison to act any differently?"

The bearded student says, "But in a mental hospital?"

The professor turns to me. "Let's ask our expert. Are the patients locked in? Do these ward aides you are describing have complete control over them?"

I say, "Actually, it's supposed to be an open ward, but I've never seen a single one of the old men try to go outside. And in my initial interview with Mr. Grimm, he said if any of the patients said they wanted to go outside, I should tell them they had to ask his permission."

"But you say none of them ever did try to go outside. Didn't you think that was odd?"

"I did think it was odd, but like I said, it was my first time on a ward. Actually, my first time in a mental hospital."

"That makes sense. But let's get back to the so-called enforcer patient. Did you see him actually hurt any of the patients on the ward?"

"Well, I did see him get ahold of one old man by the back of the neck and force his face down into his bowl of breakfast cereal. And I know that when the Growler gets ahold of the back of your neck, it hurts like hell. It feels like it's going to paralyze you."

"You have personal experience?"

"I sure do."

I'm focused on the professor's mostly impassive face, but I'm sure I heard a couple of the other students gasp.

"He took hold of the back of your neck?"

"He sure did."

"What did the people in charge of the ward do about that? Didn't they put a stop to it?"

Now I've let this discussion wander into the subject I wanted to avoid. There's no way I can explain about Eichner and the painting and all the other things I've been through since the day I walked into Cottage H.

The professor is patiently waiting for my answer, so I just quietly say, "Actually, they ordered him to do it to me. He did it to force me to sit in a chair and be quiet."

A few of the other students are whispering to each other. Are they talking about me, saying I must have done something wrong to make that happen to me? Or are they imagining themselves in the same situation?

The professor raises his hand to bring my attention back to him. "Why would they do that to a visiting student?"

Now I've done it. I don't dare get started telling him, and the whole class, about Eichner and the painting and the Israelis. But I've got to say something. The smell of tear gas in the air is not strong enough to make my eyes water, but I do sort of feel like crying. I'm feeling overwhelmed by it all, mentally exhausted. Finally, I say, "Well, I finally became sure what the Grimms were doing to the patients on their ward was wrong and threatened to report what they were doing. You know how we train a rat in behaviorism class? Well, it felt like that's what they were doing to those old men on their ward. Those old men are totally dependent on them for food and everything else, and if they do something the Grimms don't like, they initiate punishment by having the Growler grab the back of their necks. Or worse, they might send them out for electroshock therapy."

The professor holds up his hand. "Yes, in our last meeting, you did report that a patient was sent out for electroconvulsive therapy. Are you now accusing the ward aides of doing that as punishment? If that's what you're suggesting, it would be a serious misuse of that type of therapy. It might very well constitute a crime."

I hesitate. Do I want to make that accusation right out loud? But do I have any other choice? "Well, that's what it seemed like to me. You said yourself that the patient didn't seem to meet the definition of the kind of patient that would normally be sent out for that kind of shock therapy. Anyhow, I was going to report that kind of stuff to the hospital administration, and that's why they had the Growler restrain me. I only got out of Cottage H when another hospital employee, a friend of mine, came and got me out. And now he says he's going to start an investigation of what's going on at that ward."

The professor is staring at me.

Have I gone too far? Does he believe me? Or does he think I'm some kind of weirdo who he shouldn't take seriously?

He says, "Well, I think we'll all be interested in hearing how that investigation turns out, but for now, I think I'd better get back to our discussion of anti-psychotic medication."

I want to ask him one more thing, about how overdosed medication night be used in concert with reward and punishment. But I guess I've already said too much. I'd better just keep quiet and listen to his lecture.

The professor picks up right where he left off, describing the rapid transition to behavioral medicines in the field of mental health treatment, both in mental hospitals and in private psychiatric treatment. He's saying the first drugs to target depression boosted available levels of norepinephrine, a neurotransmitter. Then, he goes on to describe, with a wry smile, the marketing blitz that accompanied its introduction, including a promotional record featuring Duke Ellington and Louis Armstrong that was paid for by the drug company and distributed to doctors.

He goes on, but I'm having trouble focusing. I'm not sure if I'm just completely tired out by all that's happened in the past few days, of if it's the smell of tear gas that's somehow seeping into the room. It keeps on reminding me that dramatic things may be going on out there, possible clashes between the police and the protesters—maybe even mass arrests. I know I shouldn't even think about going out there to join the protesters. But what if I did? If I got arrested, and maybe hurt, what kind of statement would I be making? But maybe just doing it would be the point.

The professor brings my attention back, saying, "All right, that's enough for today. We'll pick up there at our next session."

The other students leave the room quickly. Are they going

out to join the anti-war protest? Or are they planning on getting off campus as quickly as possible?

I start to follow them out of the room, but Professor Spence stops me. "Listen, Scott. I'd like to know the outcome of that investigation as soon as possible. Remember, you were placed there as part of a trial program of giving independent study credit for field experience. If the hospital isn't supporting the program, if they see our students as . . . well, troublesome, we may have to cancel it."

"Oh no," I quickly say. "I think it's a great experience. In fact, it may be a lot more valuable than you . . . I mean the department, even realized. We students can learn a lot about real, day to day, mental health treatment, and the psych department can learn a lot more about what goes on out there."

"Yes, maybe more than we wanted to learn." He smiles, but I think it might be a sardonic non-smile.

I start to agree with him, but then I change my mind and say, "Well, uh, don't you think any new learning is valuable?"

He hesitates before responding, and then he nods. "Yes, you are right. If there are inappropriate treatment methods going on out there, we do need to know about it."

After he dismisses me, I walk back to my car wondering what came over me to disagree with one of my main professors like that. Has what's happened to me over the past few days changed me that much?

Maybe so. In fact, maybe I shouldn't leave campus without finding out what's going on with the anti-war demonstrations.

Instead of going to my car. I walk straight across campus to the central fountain. I don't really want to get involved in the anti-war protest, but I should at least find out what's happening.

When I get to where the protesters are, I discover that there's actually no trouble going on, at least not right now. The usual protest leaders are standing up on the ledge around the fountain, and they're shouting at the double line of police. The police are not reacting, other than staring malevolently at the students and threatening them by shaking their Billy clubs at them.

There are a few spent tear gas canisters lying around on the side-walk, so something did happen earlier, but right now, the situation seems to be in pause mode. Maybe the university administration is getting smarter and are trying not to escalate the situation. I doubt that the police will like that approach, and I'm sure the protesters don't want that either. Having seen the protesters out here every day for the past year, I'm sure they'd welcome a good confrontation, and I bet the police are always ready to bust a few more heads.

As I walk to my car, I have the sudden realization that I feel like I'm a different person than I was when this semester began. After all that's happened, everything normal now seems absurd. I'm now seeing everything in terms of motives and desires. Is that what happens when you become a psych major? Somehow I doubt that. It must just be me, the experiences I've been going through.

When I get to my car, I open the door, but I don't get in. I have a sudden memory of opening the car door for my father and helping him get in. That was before he went to that awful long-term "care" place. He was almost too weak to walk to the car, but he still wanted to get out of the house to "go see some nature." When I was a little kid, before he got sick, he often took me out to the woods so we could go for a walk. It was a fairly long drive just to get out of the city, and I liked those walks with him in the woods, but sometimes I resented the long boring drive to get there. I would have rather been out playing with my friends. Now, I regret feeling like that. How could I have been so selfish?

And what about all those old men in Cottage H? Wouldn't they like to get outside that terrible ward, if only to walk around and look at the sky? I sure hope Fred can get a serious investigation of Cottage H going so those old men can do things like that.

That thought reminds me that Fred is undoubtedly waiting to talk to me. I get into my car and head for the hospital. I'll talk to Fred, and then I'll go to the city hospital to see Jill. I sure hope her granddad recovers from his heart attack so he can get back to his little cafe, even though the only customers he will have are the demolition workers.

That reminds me that I haven't been out there in a while. With Eichner gone, and the murder found to have taken place elsewhere, there's nothing to stop them from tearing his old house down so they can get started building their fancy new shopping center.

Thirty

By the time I get to the mental hospital, lunchtime is over, so I assume Fred will be in his room. I hurry into the administration building, and tell the guard lady, "I went to see Fred. At the clinic. Thank you for what you did for him."

She waves off my praise and says, "Aw, the thanks should go to that little Puerto Rican doctor. He did some tests and figured out what was making Fred so sick. Got him treatment right away."

"Well, thank you anyway for checking up on him."

"Yeah, well we gotta keep old Fred alive, don't we? What would the kids do without him?"

"That's right," I say. "Speaking of that, has he gone back to teaching?"

"Sure he went back to teaching. No way they could stop him, but he's only doing half days until he's all better. He's in his room right now. Go on down there and see him. He'll be glad for the company."

I thank her and head for Fred's room, but she calls after me, "He got another one of them damn donut deliveries. I made him promise not to eat 'em all at once. Doctor's orders. You remind him."

I say, "Will do," and continue on down the hall to Fred's room.

I knock on his door, and I hear him call out, "Come on in."

I turn the doorknob, and sure enough, it's still not locked. Same old Fred. Why won't he take my warnings seriously?"

I go in, and as expected, he's watching his little TV with the giant box of donuts on his lap. I can see that he's already eaten most of them.

He waves a half-eaten donut at me, and says, "Hey there Scotty. Come on in and have a donut. I got two dozen of the jelly-filled kind, the kind you like."

"The kind *I* like? Two dozen of 'em, even after your doctor's warning?"

"Oh, he's just a worrywart. I feel fine now, except they half starved me to death over there in that clinic" He takes a big bite of the donut and grins at me with donut jelly all over his teeth. "What's important is what you found out. Sit down here next to me and tell me all you know."

"Well, Fred, what I know is you need to cut back on the jelly donuts."

He starts to protest, but I hold up my hand to cut him off. "No need to tell me how much better you feel. Just make sure you keep going to that doctor to get checked out. Often. But I will tell you what's gone down since I saw you last. I went back to the museum, and they said the painting must be a copy, but an old one. Maybe made when it was back in that German museum. Before the war."

Fred shakes his head. "Ha! I don't believe that for a second. It's an original van Gogh. Otherwise why would Eichner have hidden it away so carefully? And why would so many people be after it?"

"Maybe it is, maybe it isn't. Anyhow, I was going to donate it to the university museum just to get it out of my hair, but they're so convinced it's a copy, they're acting like they don't want it. I guess that means it belongs to me. That is, assuming Eichner really is gone for good."

"Good. Someday, you'll find out the truth about it, and then you'll be rich, and you'll remember to be good to your old pal Fat Freddy."

"I can't see myself ending up rich, but anyway, I cleaned it up and hung it on my wall."

"Exactly what you should have done. Next, you'll invite me over to your place to see it."

"Sure thing. But don't you have some things to tell me about? The investigation?"

"I sure do. I spoke to the head nurse, and she said you can go to work for me. She said you should get the hell off that terrible old men's ward and help me with my students."

"I think I'd like that, Fred. But what about those poor old men at Cottage H? Isn't she going to do anything about what the Grimms are doing to them?"

"Well, that's more complicated. That's the word she used, 'complicated.'"

"Complicated? What did she mean by that? Isn't she going to do anything about it?"

Fred opens his box of donuts, and seems to be deciding which one to eat next. He chooses one and holds it out to me. "Hey, don't look so down, Scotty. Here, have a donut."

I wave it off. "What aren't you saying, Fred? That she doesn't want to do anything about what's going on over at Cottage H?"

"Well, she told me the Grimms have a lot of power in this institution. The aides are the ones who actually run this place, and the Grimms have been here longer than just about anybody. There's a kind of underground word-of-mouth telegraph system here, and the word is out that you're a troublemaker."

"Me? Now I've become the problem?"

"Well, you've become *their* problem. I'll tell you something, Scott. You'd better be careful around any of the aides. You won't believe the things I hear from my students. They told me most of the aides claim to have hip problems, so they can carry around big heavy canes. You can imagine what they use those canes for."

"You're saying Cottage H isn't the only bad ward? Is punishment the way all the aides control their patients?"

Fred shrugs. "That's what my students tell me. Don't forget those aides are alone on those wards with a lot of patients. And they don't make much money."

"What are you implying Fred? That they only hire mean people who might hurt the patients?"

Fred shrugs again. "Well, that's what my students think. But then, they've never had a very good opinion of the aides."

"So, the Grimms are going to get away with it. Nothing is going to change."

Fred takes another big bite from his jelly donut, and then he reaches out to land a light punch on my shoulder. "Maybe. What's important is that you're gonna get to come work with me. We'll have loads of fun. Like I said, you'll like my kids. Most of them aren't any problem at all. They've just been through some hard times. You're just the kind of model they need, a sharp college student."

"Right now, Fred, I'm not feeling all that sharp. I'm kind of worn out by everything that's happened. And now you're telling me how things work in this place. It's pretty depressing."

Fred nods as if he's agreeing with me, but then he says, "It's just the way it is, Scotty. Sometimes we just have to accept that. I stick to my little domain, my schoolroom, and try to help the kids as best I can. You can help me do that. Okay?"

Even though I'm feeling depressed and angry at the same time, I know he's right. I nod to let him know I agree with him. I have to admit I really am looking forward to working with him to try to help those kids.

Fred's frown turns into a grin. "All right! Now let's kick back and have some donuts."

I accept a donut, but I'm still not happy with what he's telling me. Today, at the university, the police were using clubs and tear gas to control the protesting students, and now he's telling me the aides here are using their club-like canes to control their patients. Am I naive to be shocked at that? Is it just how the world works? Have I been too out of it to notice?

Fred continues telling me about how great it will be to work together in his classroom, and I'm sure he's right, but I'm feeling distracted and restless.

Finally, I thank him for the donut, and tell him I'd better go visit Jill and her grandfather at the city hospital. He tries to get me to take a couple of donuts with me to "tide me over" until supper time. At first I refuse his repeated offers, but then I change my mind and take them. At least it will keep him from eating all of them.

On my way out of the building, I give the two jelly donuts to the guard lady at the front desk. She thanks me and says, "I hope he's not going to eat all the rest of them tonight. Is he?"

"Probably," I say and head out the door to my car.

Thirty-One

At the city hospital, I realize I'm going to have a hard time finding Jill. I don't even know her last name. That upsets me. Why didn't I think to ask her that? Has everything that's happened got me so distracted I can't even remember to ask such an obvious question? But maybe it's because I feel like I got to know her so well that night we searched Eichner's old house, it didn't seem like she needed a last name—she was just . . . Jill. I remember lifting her up so she could get ahold of the trap door in Eichner's ceiling. She seemed so light.

I tell the receptionist I'm looking for a young woman who is here with her grandfather who is a patient in this hospital. She patiently listens to my rambling description of Jill, and then she asks me why her grandfather is in the hospital. I tell her he's recovering from heart surgery.

She says, "That means he'll be up on the second floor. Somebody up there will know who you're looking for."

Sure enough, the nurse in the second-floor nurse's station knows exactly who I'm talking about, the cute young girl who stays with her grandfather, day and night. She directs me to the correct room.

When I get there, I find Jill sitting in a chair next to her grandfather, reading to him. He's propped up in his bed, but he doesn't seem to be listening to her very carefully.

I stay in the doorway to watch her read. She's very focused on the story, reading it with passion and changing her voice to reflect the speech of the different characters in the story.

I clear my throat, and that makes Jill look up. She jumps up and runs to give me a hug. Then, she leads me to her grandfather's bedside and introduces me.

He grandfather looks me over and says, "So this is the famous Scott. She talks so much about how great you are I thought maybe you'd be wearing a superman's cape."

Jill flushes red and says, "Oh Granddad, all I did was tell you how he works in a mental hospital helping people."

"Yeah, and how he found a famous painting that's been lost since the war."

I jump in with, "I've heard a lot about you too, sir. Jill tells me you've been having a rough time of it."

For some reason, he laughs, and then he says, "You might say that. But I'm just about better now and ready to get back to work."

"Right," I say. "The last time I was out there, they've got all the houses pretty well cleared off now. It looks like they may be about ready to start building."

He looks at Jill and says, "What did I tell you, Jill. Soon, there will be so many workers coming into our place we'll have to beat 'em off with a stick."

I smile and say, "I agree with you, sir. It looks like it's going to be quite a big project over there."

My words seem to make him happy, but then he says, "I'm sure you didn't come here to see me. Why don't you two young people go for a walk while I take a nap."

Out in the hallway, Jill tells me she's happy that her grand-dad is feeling so much better, but she's worried that he'll try to come back too quickly and think he should come help her at the cafe.

I agree with her and suggest that maybe he should stay in the hospital a little longer.

"No," she says, "there's no holding him back now. They say he can go home tomorrow if he wants to, and he really wants to."

"Okay, then will I see you at the cafe tomorrow?"

She hesitates, then says, "I guess I should at least go in for the lunch crowd. We sure could use the money. Heart surgery isn't cheap. Thank goodness President Johnson was able to push through Medicare, or I don't know what we would have done. But we still have to pay part of the hospital bill."

I reach out to touch her hand. "I sure wish the painting, our painting, would have been an original van Gogh. Then we'd have plenty."

"We? Are you saying it belongs to us now?"

"Well, we found it, didn't we? And now that Eichner is gone, I guess you might say it doesn't belong to anybody. Besides, he stole it from that museum in the first place."

She shakes her head. "Be that as it may, it's not up to you to worry about our bills. We'll do fine. Just tell me you'll be there tomorrow. At the cafe, after lunchtime."

"I sure will. We can talk more then."

"Right. And then I want to come see the painting again. I think about it a lot."

"Come to my place? Oh, I mean, yes. For sure. You should come to my place and see how nice it looks now that I've cleaned it up."

She squeezes my hand, and says, "It's a date. Now I'd better get back in granddad's room. I'm still not sure he's well enough to go home tomorrow."

"He seems to be doing fine. I mean for a man who had a heart attack."

"I sure hope so. Anyhow, see you tomorrow."

Thirty-Two

On my way back to my apartment, I think about what Jill said about coming to visit me. Once again, it makes me think about the fact that not one person has ever come to my place. I guess that's my fault. While my father was sick, I didn't really want to make any new friends. By the time he died, I guess I'd kind of gotten out of the habit of talking to people. And if you don't talk to people, you don't make friends. Now both Jill and Fred say they want to come visit me, and I have to admit I'm looking forward to it. It's one more thing that shows I'm changing. But into what? Am I going back to who I was before? I don't think so. I guess I'm evolving into a new self. Do I like my new self? I think I do.

As I pull into my usual parking place next to my apartment, I see the old Jewish woman, still out there doing her incessant sweeping.

She stares at me as I go into my apartment. I'd like to talk to her, to maybe find out if anyone else has come by, but she ignores me and goes off sweeping in another direction. Fine with me. I'm ready to get into my apartment and try to relax after the long weird day I've had. I especially don't want to think anymore about the bad stuff that's going on at the mental hospital. I think I'll just spend some time looking at the painting and be thankful that Jill is all right after all.

As soon as I've closed the door and locked it, I turn to the wall to see how the painting looks in this late afternoon light.

There's nothing but a blank wall. The painting is gone!

How can that be?

At first, I think maybe the tape came loose, and it fell to the floor. But it's not there. Obviously, somebody came into my apartment and took it. I look toward the door to see if there is any sign that it was pried open, but there's nothing. The same with my window—it's still securely locked. Does somebody have a key? The managers of these apartments undoubtedly do, but I don't even know who they are. My mother was the one who rented this apartment, and she pays the rent.

My mind immediately turns to that old Jewish sweeper woman. She's always out there. If somebody broke in, she must have seen them.

I hurry outside, and she's standing right there outside my door, leaning on her broom, as if she was waiting for me to come out.

"Listen, ma'am, somebody broke into my place and stole something of mine. Did you see anybody?"

"Now, now," young man," she says. "You know painting not belong you."

All I can do is stand there and stare at her. She knows about the painting? And she's saying it doesn't belong to me? What does she know about it? She said something earlier about somebody looking for me, and she mentioned the painting and Eichner back then also. Is she saying the painting still belongs to Eichner?

"Wait," she says. "I get him. He explain."

She goes to the door of the apartment next to mine and raps on it.

A young, dark-haired man immediately comes out and steps forward to shake my head. I recognize him! He was the man who dragged Eichner out of the dorm while his partner held me back.

"I don't want to shake your hand," I say. "I know who you are. You kidnapped Mr. Eichner."

"No, we didn't *kidnap* Eichner. We arrested him. Let me explain. My name is Steinberg. I work for the government of Israel, and we've been looking for Eichner for a long time. We finally tracked him down, hiding in a ward at the local mental hospital, the ward where you are working."

"I'm not working there. I'm only a student. And I only met Eichner as a patient there. So why are you two spying on me?" I point to the old sweeper woman who's leaning on her broom. She seems to be enjoying listening to us talk.

Steinberg nods, looking grim. "I'm sorry about that, son. But we had to be sure you weren't working with Eichner, and when we found out the apartment next to yours was available, we took it."

"So you moved right in and sent your old mother out to pretend to be a sweeper so she could watch my comings and goings."

"She's not my mother. She works for the same government agency that I do. My mother is deceased. At least I think she is. Some time ago, she lived right next door to Eichner, in this very town. She disappeared, and I was sure Eichner had something to do with it. So you see, catching Eichner was personal for me."

Uh oh. So this is Mrs. Steinberg's son, the one Eichner said came looking for her. Should I tell him the story Eichner told me about how he killed her? Or would that make me an accomplice?

No, I did report the story to Mr. Grimm, and he laughed it off. Said Eichner was just a teller of "tall tales."

"Listen, young man. I can see it worries you that you may have been dealing with a murderer, but none of that matters now. Eichner will either be executed or spend the rest of his life in prison for the crimes he committed during the war."

"Crimes he committed? During the war?"

"Yes. He worked as a guard at a Nazi concentration camp near Magdeburg, Germany. He was complicit in the murders of many, many people."

So he knows about Magdeburg. Does he also know about the art museum there? "Be that as it may, Mr. Steinberg, you had no right to steal my painting. It was you who stole it, wasn't it?"

"That painting doesn't belong to you, son. It belongs to the heirs of the German Jewish family that it was stolen from, a family who lost their parents at the hands of the Nazis. The Nazis stole that painting, and it will be returned to its rightful owners. That will probably be the last you will hear about it. Generally, when these old families get their art back, they keep it secret. For fear of robbers. "

I'm trying to understand the implications of what he's saying. "You mean it's a real van Gogh? An original?"

"It is. Eichner's brother stole it from a museum in that same German town. He worked there as a guard, and he took a number of paintings from that museum during the war. According to our sources in Germany, after his brother died in an Allied air raid, Eichner got the paintings his brother had been systematically stealing from the museum. He managed to ship them to this country, and after the war, he emigrated here and got them out of storage and sold them off. We've been able to retrieve most of them, but we thought he might have more. We assumed he might have them hidden somewhere in his house, but we were never able to find them. That's when you came into the picture. We saw you and the girl break into his house. I almost caught you that night, but you slipped away from me. Eventually, I found out who you were, and I searched your apartment. but found nothing. I was still sure you got something from Eichner's house, and that's why you ran. Since then, we've been watching you. Finally, yesterday, you showed up with the painting. We were about to arrest you, but Mr. and Mrs. Grimm, our contacts at the mental hospital, assured us that you were not part of any conspiracy. We have decided to accept their explanation that you were just a naive student who got fooled by Eichner."

"I may only be a student, but I'm not naive. I knew I couldn't believe everything Eichner told me. In fact, when he told me about—"

Steinberg holds up one hand to stop me. "No need to explain, son. We believe you are not complicit. We'll leave you alone now. He nods to the old sweeper woman, and she surprises me by handing me her broom. She winks at me, and then both of them turn away and walk to a black car that's parked down near the end of the apartment building.

Standing on the sidewalk with her broom in my hand, I watch them drive away. I'm still having trouble believing all he told me. Can it be true that I carried an original van Gogh around inside my shirt? That I cleaned it with my own spit?

I throw down the broom and hurry inside my apartment. I lock the door, and then I turn to look at the bare wall that still has pieces of tape on it from where the painting was.

I go to sit down on my bed, still staring at the wall where the painting was. Oh well, I guess there's no use brooding about it. At one time, I was planning to give the painting to the university museum anyhow, just to be rid of it. Now that it's gone, I hope I'm no longer in danger. And Jill and Fred should also be safe now. At least I hope that's true. I hope whoever was after it will soon find out it has been returned to Germany.

I notice my stack of textbooks. It reminds me that I'm still behind in my studies. I'd better get back to acting like who I really am, a student. I'll get to finish my independent study at the mental hospital in Fred's classroom, which should be a much better learning environment for me. And I'll get to spend a lot of time with Fred. I think I'm going to like that.

And despite all the weird things that happened, I have to be grateful for one thing: I made a very special new friend, Jill. I sure hope she'll still want to come here and spend some time with me. In fact, I hope she'll want to spend a lot of time with me. We can sit here together on this very bed and talk about the painting and the big adventure we had together.

You know, after staying alone for so long after my father died, maybe it's time for me to re-emerge into the world. Assuming that is, I don't get drafted and sent off to get killed in Vietnam.

www.ingramcontent.com/pod-product-compliance
Lightning Source LLC
Chambersburg PA
CBHW070825120626
46556CB00002B/656